LOVE'S DILEMMA

LOVE'S MAGIC SERIES BOOK 20

BETTY MCLAIN

This book is dedicated to my daughter, Amanda, whose skills, creativity and dedication have solved the dilemma of what to do with all the books I have written. Thanks, Amanda.

CAST OF CHARACTERS

Cendera – Town of Vigilantes
Alex Avorn – Avorn Security
Mariam Avorn – Alex's wife
Mark Avorn – Alex's brother – half owner of Avorn Security –
Dottie Sue Flinn Avorn – Mark's wife – former resident of Cendera
Darrin Semp – Mariam's brother – Building manager at Avorn Acres
Becky Rand Semp – Darrin's wife – former resident of Cendera
Phillip Sarnes – Alex's partner in cabinet factory
Taylor Aris Sarnes – Phillip's wife – former resident of Cendera
Salvadori (Sal) Mase – Avorn agent – friend and partner of Micky
Micky Ansel – Avorn Agent – friend and partner of Sal
Selma Dolan – Former resident of Cendera – Living with Sal's
parents and going to school
Jayann Newsom – Mariam's doctor
Dr. Parks – Avorn's company doctor
James Kirk – Avorn security guard – friend of Sal's
Trey and Lori Loden – Avorn agents – Friends of Avorn family
Andrew Salto and Nelson Baker – Avorn Agents
Brenda - Alex's Assistant

Klark Aris – Taylor Sarnes' dad - Jarrick Rand – Becky Semp's dad

Lynn Clark – Front desk – third floor

Frank and Drako – Front desk at door to Avorn building – different shifts

Sandor (Sandy) Mase – Former Avorn Agent – Fitness Instructor at college and at Avorn

Minnie Mase – Sandy's wife

Albert Dolan – Selma's father

Phebe and Cameron Banks – Selma's Aunt and Uncle in Cendera

Cecil and Clarence Banks – Selma's young cousins in Cendera.

Stacy Clark – Micky's true love

CHAPTER 1

Selma closed her schoolbook as she finished her homework. She put her book aside and went into the kitchen where Mrs. Mase was preparing the evening meal.

"I'm finished with my homework. What can I help with?" asked Selma.

Mrs. Mase smiled at Selma. "You can set the table," replied Mrs. Mase. Her eyes followed Selma as she took the dishes from the cabinet and started setting them on the table. "She is such a sweet girl," thought Mrs. Mase. "I am so glad Sal brought her to me." She knew Sal was interested in Selena and she was happy with his choice. Both of her boys had made great choices in their life partners, she thought with satisfaction.

Selma was from the town of Cendera, but she did not show the vigilante powers the other residents had. Selma had hidden her powers from everyone. She had felt out of place and very much wanted to leave. Her chance to leave came when Sal accompanied Alex Avorn's group to Cendera for the weddings of three girls from Cendera to the young men their guardian angels had picked for them. Mark, one of the men was Alex's brother. Darrin, another of the men was the brother of Mariam Avorn, Alex's wife.

While the Avorn group was in Cendera, and Selma had seen Sal, she recognized him from her magic mirror. She knew they were meant to be together, so Selma had taken a chance and asked Sal to help her to leave. The council talked to her and gave their approval and Sal called Mrs. Mase and arranged for Selma to stay with his parents and finish high school. Even though their guardian angels and the magic mirror had indicated Sal and Selma were meant for each other, they both realized, Selma was too young for any serious relationship. During the four months Selma had been at the Mase home, Sal and Micky came by regularly to see how Selma was doing. They were all pleased with how the situation was progressing.

Selma looked forward to the times when Sal came by. She was quiet when he was around, but her eyes followed him, and she was waiting for the day when Sal decided she was old enough for a closer relationship. Sal's eyes followed Selma also. He was drawn to her, but he was trying to give her time to adjust to his presence. Micky sometimes teased him about his infatuation with Selma.

"You can set four extra places," said Mrs. Mase. "Sal and Micky are going to be stopping by. Sandy and Minnie are coming by, also. When I told Sal, Sandy and Minnie would be here and we were having pot roast, he decided to make it in time to eat."

Selma laughed. "He does love your pot roast," she agreed as she hugged the thought of seeing Sal soon to her.

Mrs. Mase smiled. "I think he misses spending time with Sandy. They are all so busy, they don't have time to get together like they used to. Sandy is busy with his new job and with Minnie taking classes at the college, they spend most evenings at home. They are still newlyweds, after all."

Selma smiled as she thought about Minnie and Sandy. They had visited with Mr. and Mrs. Mase many times in the four months Selma had lived with the Mases. Selma and Minnie had become friends, and Selma enjoyed having Minnie around to ask for advice.

She was living in a different environment than she was used to in Cendera. Minnie guidance had been very welcome.

"Hello, everyone," called Sandy as he and Minnie entered the door from the garage.

Minnie hurried over to give Mrs. Mase a hug. She turned and hugged Selma also.

"I hope you don't mind Sandy inviting us to eat your pot roast," said Minnie with a smile. "When he heard what you were cooking, his mouth started watering. I am sure he could taste it, just thinking about it." Minnie and Selma laughed, and Mrs. Mase smiled with satisfaction. She was happy her boys loved her cooking.

"You are both welcome anytime. I love having you here," said Mrs. Mase.

Minnie gave Mrs. Mase another hug before she turned to Selma and started helping her place the dishes on the table. "How are your classes going?" she asked.

"They are going very well," replied Selma. "I am ready for finals week after next. I wanted to ask you about the senior prom. The other students are all excited about it, and all the girls talk about is what they are going to wear and who has asked them to the dance."

Minnie smiled. "It is a very important time for most of the students. It is a celebration of the end of their high school years."

Selma frowned. "Do they expect everyone to go, even if they don't have a date?"

Minnie shook her head. "You don't have to go if you don't want to." Minnie looked at Selma thoughtfully. "Hasn't anyone asked you to the dance?"

Selma looked down shyly. "A couple of boys asked me, but I turned them down."

"Why?" asked Sandy. He had been listening while the girls talked.

Selma glanced at Sandy and shook her head. "I didn't feel it was right to go out with them," she said.

The door opened and Sal and Micky entered.

3

"Hi, everyone," said Sal as he stopped and hugged his mom.

He noticed Sandy was looking at Selma and frowning. "What's going on?" he asked.

Sandy glanced at Sal and smiled. "I was just trying to find out why Selma doesn't think she should accept a date to her prom."

Sal looked at Selma, startled. Selma looked at him shyly.

Sal went over and took her hand. "Do you want to go to the prom?" he asked.

Selma looked up at him and nodded.

"Will you let me take you?" he asked.

Sandy and Minnie looked at Sal and smiled. Micky grinned and turned to glance at Mrs. Mase. She was watching then with a satisfied look on her face.

Mr. Mase entered the garage door and looked startled to see a room full when he entered. He gave everyone a look and went over to kiss Mrs. Mase. "We have guests for supper. I see," he said.

Sal ignored then all as he kept Selma's hand in his. He looked at her inquiringly. "Will you go with me?" he asked again.

Selma nodded. Sal grinned and gave Selma a brief hug. "Great, just let me know when it is and the color of your dress."

Selma gazed at him in puzzlement. "Why do you need to know the color of my dress?" she asked.

"So, he can get you a corsage," said Minnie.

"Oh," whispered Selma. "I've never had anyone get me a corsage before," she said.

Sal smiled. "It's high time you did," he said and squeezed her hand. Selma gave him a smile and squeezed his hand gently. Sal smiled back at her and held onto her hand.

"Let's eat," said Mrs. Mase. While everyone had been listening to and watching Sal and Selma, she and Micky had been putting food on the table.

They all turned to the table and started taking seats. Sal held onto Selma's hand and seated her in a chair next to him before releasing her. Selma smiled at him as she took her seat and he smiled back at her and rubbed a finger over her cheek. Sal took his seat and ignored the smiles and knowing looks he received from his family and Micky.

Minnie glanced at Selma and smiled. "Do you want to go shopping with me tomorrow after class? We can look for a prom dress," she asked.

"I would like that," agreed Selma.

"Okay," agreed Minnie. "I'll pick you up at school and we can go from there."

"Thanks, I will look forward to it" said Selma.

"I have been looking for an excuse for a shopping trip," said Minnie with a glance at Sandy. Sandy smiled at her. "You girls enjoy yourselves," he said.

Minnie reached for his hand and gave it a squeeze. "We will," she promised.

They had finished eating their dinner and dug into a chocolate cake for desert. When they were done, the group started clearing the table. They insisted Mrs. Mase go and relax and let them do the cleaning. She and Mr. Mase went into the front room and turned on the television.

There was a knock and they heard Mr. Mase go and open the door. Minnie was surprised to hear her brother Bobby's voice.

"Hi, I saw Sandy's car out front and I thought I would stop and say hello," said Bobby as Mr. Mase let him in the door.

"Hello, Bobby. Sandy and Minnie are in the kitchen. How have you been. I haven't seen you in a while," said Mr. Mase.

"I have been busy," said Bobby. "Mom asked me to stop by and check on the house while she and Arnie are on their cruise. She was very excited when Arnie presented her with tickets for a cruise. She had always dreamed of going on a cruise, but she never had a chance before."

"Hello, Bobby," greeted Mrs. Mase.

Bobby went over to Mrs. Mase and gave her a hug. "It's good to see you," said Bobby.

"You should have come by earlier and had supper with us," said Mrs. Mase.

"Yes, I can smell your pot roast. I'm sorry I missed it," said Bobby.

"You missed chocolate cake, also," said Mrs. Mase with a twinkle in her eye.

"Oh no," said Bobby with a downcast look. "I'll have to come earlier next time," he said.

Mr. and Mrs. Mase both laughed.

"If you have trouble getting by, just call. I will be glad to check on the house for you," said Mrs. Mase.

"That is sweet of you," said Bobby. "I may take you up on it."

"Hello, Bobby," said Sandy entering the room. "I thought I heard your voice."

"Hi," said Bobby going over to give Sandy a hug. "I saw your car, and I wanted to ask Minnie something."

"She's in the kitchen. She will be here as soon as they finish cleaning up," said Sandy.

"Have a seat, Bobby," encouraged Mr. Mase.

"Thanks," said Bobby. "I think I will join the others in the kitchen so I can talk to Minnie. It was great seeing you both."

"Don't be a stranger. Stop by anytime," encouraged Mr. Mase.

"Thanks, I will," said Bobby as he followed Sandy to the kitchen.

"Look who's here," said Sandy as they entered the kitchen.

"Bobby," said Minnie with a big smile as she went to give Bobby a hug.

"Hi, Sis, I saw Sandy's car when I was checking on Mom's house and I wanted to ask you about the tunnel," said Bobby.

"What about it?" asked Minnie looking at him curiously.

"You said it was too small for any of us guys to get through." Minnie was nodding. "You locked the door going into my room," Minnie nodded again. "I was wondering if I could get you to go through the tunnel and unlock the door. I have some things stored in the room at the bottom of the stairs, and I would like to get them while Mom and Arnie are gone. If I try to get them while they are there, they might discover the tunnel," concluded Bobby.

Sandy was shaking his head. "I don't think that is a good idea. I don't think Minnie should be going through the tunnel again," he objected.

Minnie put her hand on his arm. "It's perfectly safe. There were no cave ins. It is just too small for you guys. You built it when you were very young."

"I just don't like the idea of you going through it by yourself," said Sandy. "You were so scared when you came through it. I don't like to think of it scaring you again."

"I won't be scared. I know you guys are all here waiting for me," said Minnie patting his arm reassuringly.

"I could go with you," said Selma.

Minnie looked at her and grinned. "You wouldn't be scared?" she asked.

Selma shook her head. "It sounds like an adventure."

Sal took Selma's hand. "Are you sure?" he asked.

Selma smiled. "I am very sure. Where is the tunnel?" she asked.

"The door is in our club house. The tunnel goes to Bobby's clubhouse under his room next door," said Minnie.

Selma looked around the group surrounding her. "You guys must have had an awesome childhood," she said wistfully.

"It was pretty awesome," agreed Sal. The others nodded agreement with large smiles.

"When do you want me to unlock the door?" asked Minnie.

"How about now?" asked Bobby. "We are all here. Sal and I can go over to Mom's house and wait for you. Sandy and Micky can watch from this end."

"I have some flashlights in the car," said Sal. "I'll get them and meet you in the clubhouse."

They all went out the door to the garage. Sal headed to the front and his car. The others went through the back door of the garage and to the clubhouse.

Minnie sighed when they were all inside and she looked around. The place looked much smaller with four well-built guys inside. It had been made for children.

Sal brought the flashlights. He also brought some walkie talkies for them to keep in touch with the girls. He went over and opened the door to the tunnel and flashed the light inside. He looked at Selma, standing by his side. "Are you sure you want to do this?" he asked.

Selma smiled and nodded. "I'll be fine," she said.

Sal gave her hand a squeeze and handed her one of the flashlights. Leaning forward he kissed her gently. "I'll be waiting at the other end. Be careful." Sal gave the other flashlight and a walkie talkie to Minnie. He gave Sandy the other walkie talkie and stood waiting for the girls to start their trip. Sal held onto Selma's hand while waiting for Sandy to finish hugging Minnie.

"I will see you at the other end," promised Selma. She could hardly breathe. Sal had kissed her. She hugged the memory tightly inside as she waited for Minnie to start the trip through the tunnel.

Minnie was patiently listening to Sandy's instructions. Finally, she kissed him and started into the tunnel. Selma followed her inside.

"We may have to bend down in places, but I don't think we will have to crawl," said Minnie, leading the way down the tunnel. They went slowly and flashed the light around. Selma was amazed at how well built the tunnel was, considering it had been built by children.

"This is much better than the last time I came through," remarked Minnie. "I was so, frightened, I couldn't enjoy the trip."

"I'm glad you let me come with you," said Selma.

"I am glad you are here. It makes it nicer to have some-one to talk to," she said.

"Are you girls alright?" asked Sandy on the walkie talkie.

"We are fine," said Minnie. "We are almost to the end. Why don't you head on over and meet us at the house?" suggested Minnie.

"Okay, I'll see you there," responded Sandy.

Minnie sighed and smiled. Selma laughed. "He doesn't want you out of his sight," she said.

Minnie laughed softly. "I know. I love it. He is relaxing some since he started his new job. We both are busy, but he is still very protective. Sal will probably be the same way. It is just that way with the Mase brothers."

"I think it is sweet," said Selma.

Minnie laughed and agreed with her.

They emerged in a room with stairs going up. Minnie and Selma shined their lights around. They were both curious. Minnie had been in such a hurry when she had come through before, she didn't take time to look around.

"Are you here?" asked Sandy.

Minnie smiled and turned to the stairs. She quickly went up and unlocked the door under the chest in Bobby's closet. Bobby pushed the button and the chest slid to the side leaving a door for them to come down the stairs. The guys all came down the stairs. Sandy hugged and kissed Minnie and Sal hugged Selma. Bobby and Micky stood looking around.

Minnie looked around. This place sure shrinks with all of you guys in here," she said.

Bobby went over to some large plastic containers under the stairs. He took one and started up the stairs. Micky took another and followed him. They sat the containers down in Bobby's room. Sandy came up with a container. Minnie followed him with Selma behind her. Sal came up last. Bobby went over and pushed the hidden button to close the entrance.

Selma looked around wide eyed. "It was amazing," she said smiling at Sal. Sal smiled back at her. He had a hold of her hand again. He didn't seem to want to turn her loose.

"Are you going through these now?" asked Minnie.

"No," answered Bobby. "I'm going to take them to my apartment so I can take my time going through them and deciding what I want to keep," said Bobby.

"Let's get them loaded in your car," said Micky picking up one container and starting for the door. Bobby and Sal took the other two and followed him out. Bobby opened his trunk and they placed two containers inside. Bobby opened the back door and placed the third container on the back seat.

After locking the doors Bobby turned to the guys. He looked at Minnie. "Thanks, Sis, for going through the tunnel. I hope it wasn't too bad."

"You are welcome. It was fine with Selma there." She flashed Selma a big smile.

Selma smiled back when Bobby looked at her. "Thanks, Selma," he said.

"I loved it," said Selma with a flush on her cheeks. She handed her flashlight to Sal.

Minnie took the walkie talkie from Sandy and took her flashlight and the walkie talkies to Sal. "I'll put these in our car and join you guys inside so we can say goodnight to Mom and Dad," said Sal.

They all turned and headed back to the Mase house. They went inside and were soon joined by Sal.

Mr. and Mrs. Mase looked up with a smile when everyone entered the room.

"Thanks for a great meal," said Sandy going over and giving his Mom a hug. "Minnie and I have to go. It is going to be an early day tomorrow."

"I'm glad you all came by," said Mrs. Mase returning his hug and turning to Hug Minnie.

"I'll see you tomorrow when I drop Selma off after our shopping trip," said Minnie.

"I need to be going, too," said Bobby. "It was good to see you both. He shook Mr. Mase's hand and hugged Mrs. Mase before following Minnie and Sandy outside.

Sal and Micky followed them outside. Selma and Minnie were firming up their plans for their shopping trip while they all said goodbye.

They stood on the porch and waved as Bobby and Sandy drove away. Micky turned and went back inside. Sal and Selma lingered on the porch. Selma glanced at Sal shyly. He was watching her and smiled at her glance.

"I'm glad you agreed to go to the prom with me," said Sal.

"Thank you for asking me," said Selma.

Sal leaned forward and kissed her gently. Selma sighed and Sal rested his forehead gently against hers. "There was no way I was going to let some other guy take my girl to the prom," protested Sal.

Selma grinned. "I am your girl?" she asked.

Sal looked at her. "Yes, you are. Aren't you?" he asked'

Selma nodded. "Yes," she whispered.

"You have fun shopping with Minnie tomorrow, but you girls be careful," said Sal.

"We will," promised Selma. "We had better go in so you and Micky can leave," said Selma.

Sal kissed her once more before opening the door and returning inside.

"We had better go," Sal said to Micky. Micky nodded and rose to follow Sal after he told Sal's parents goodnight.

Selma watched them leave with one last glance and a smile from Sal. After they were gone, Selma said goodnight and taking her schoolbooks, she went to her room. She lay her books down and flopped down on the bed. It was a good thing she had finished her homework. She would never have been able to study after Sal had kissed her. All she could think about was Sal and his kisses.

Micky looked over at Sal and grinned.

"What?" asked Sal.

"Micky chuckled. "Nothing, I'm glad you found someone that makes you happy," he said. "I wish I could find my mate."

"She's out there," said Sal. "You just have to be patient and listen to your guardian angel."

"I keep waiting. So far, I have not heard a word about love from my guardian angel," said Micky.

Sal shook his head. "I was losing hope when Selma appeared in my life. It will be the same for you. Don't lose hope."

Micky looked at Sal and grinned. "I won't," he promised.

Mr. Mase sat beside his wife on the sofa. He had his arm around her, and they were laughing at a comedian on the television. He looked down at her and smiled.

"The boys are both lucky to find girls almost as great as their Mom," said Mr. Mase with a smile.

Mrs. Mase grinned up at him. "I am very happy for them. I am glad they made such good choices. It is always worrying when your children are old enough to start looking for a mate."

"You set a good example for them. They were looking for someone as sweet as their mom," said Mr. Mase.

Mrs. Mase smiled at him and leaning forward, kissed him gently. "They had you as an example of how a gentleman was supposed to treat the love of his life."

Mr. Mase smiled with satisfaction. "We are very blessed," he agreed. They settled back to finish watching their show.

Meanwhile, Selma had fallen asleep with a smile on her face. She was dreaming about dancing with Sal. He was holding her close and smiling down at her. She had on a beautiful sea green dress and there was a lovely sea green flower on her wrist. In her dream, she and Sal were gazing into each other's eyes and smiling. The look on his face made her toes curl. Selma hugged the wonderful feelings close and dreamed on. She did not think about her schoolbooks at all. They were where she had dropped them when she had entered her room.

CHAPTER 2

Selma was waiting at the gym entrance the next day when Minnie arrived to pick her up. Minnie had told her about the back way into the school. Minnie knew about the entrance because her mom had worked as a janitor for the school for many years. By meeting at the back, they avoided the long lines of parents there to pick up their children.

Minnie stopped and smiled at Selma as she entered the front passenger seat. "Ready for shopping?" she asked.

"Oh, yes," said Selma excitedly. "Where are we going?"

"I thought we could try the mall. There are several dress shops we can check out, and then we can stop at the food court and get something to eat," said Minnie.

"That sounds great," said Selma sitting back in her seat and smiling happily.

Minnie parked close to the front door of the mall. She and Selma walked into the front door and Selma stopped to look around. Minnie smiled at the look of excitement on her face.

"Do you have malls in Cendera?" she asked.

Selma shook her head. "No, we only have small stores.

Everything is brought in. Everything is free to anyone who is a Cendera resident. We do have a seamstress to make custom orders for us."

"Wow," exclaimed Minnie. "You don't have to pay to shop."

"No," explained Selma. "Cendera owns a diamond mine and an emerald mine. The money is used for all the residents. Everything needed is provided by the town council. If a house is needed, the council sees to the building of it. Everyone brings their extra products to be shared."

Minnie shook her head. "It sounds like a dream come true," she said as she guided Selma toward the first dress shop.

"It is much nicer to be able to wander around the mall and see all the stores. Even if we do not buy anything, it is fun just to look," said Selma looking around.

Minnie nodded. She gave Selma a big smile. "I love shopping. It is fun just to wander around and see all the people rushing about. I especially like shopping in the mall. There are so many stores in one place. I can take my time and find what I need. The only thing we can't buy here is groceries. We have to go to the grocery store for them."

"I thought you said there was a food court," said Selma.

"There is, but it is prepared food. There are tables where you can sit and eat here, or you can eat it while walking around looking," explained Minnie.

They entered the dress shop and wandered around looking at the dresses on display. Selma and Minnie stopped to look at several dresses, but Minnie could tell by looking at Selma's face, she was not really liking any of the dresses.

"Let's go to another store and see what they have," suggested Minnie.

"Okay," agreed Selma as she followed Minnie out the door and down the mall to the next dress shop.

They didn't find anything they liked in the next store. Since the food court was next, they decided to get a slice of pizza and sit at a table and eat it while watching everyone shopping.

When they went to pay for the pizza, Minnie showed Selma how to use her debit card. The council of Cendera had set up an account for her, but she had never used the card until now.

After they had their pizza and sat at a table to eat, Selma thought about when she had first moved in with the Mases. Sal and Micky had taken her to the Mase home on their return from Cendera. They had dropped Alex and Mariam off at the Avorn building before taking Selma and introducing her to Mr. and Mrs. Mase. It was love at first sight for Selma. It did not take long for the Mases to become like the family she had not had since her mom's death.

Selma had tried to pay the Mases for staying with them. They had refused any payment. Mrs. Mase had told her they were not charging for Selma staying with them. She told Selma seeing her get her education was payment enough. Selma tried to help all Mrs. Mase would let her, but Mrs. Mase insisted school came first.

Minnie laughed and drew Selma's attention. When she looked up, she saw Minnie watching a little girl dancing around. Selma smiled. The girl was very small, about four or five. She was enjoying showing off. Her mother looked around and saw her drawing all the attention to herself and hurried to take her to her seat to eat. The girl looked at Minnie and Selma and grinned as her mother sat her at the table. Both girls smiled back at her.

"What a cutie," said Minnie.

"Yes," agreed Selma. "She's sure not bashful."

Minnie looked at Selma. "Were you bashful as a child?" she asked

Selma thought for a minute, then shook her head. "I was not so much bashful, but I tried not to draw attention to myself. I never knew what to expect if I was the center of attention."

"It must have been hard," said Minnie. "I know what you mean about not drawing attention to yourself. I did the same thing after

Mom married Arnie." Minnie looked down as she thought about the time before Sandy had rescued her.

"Did you not like your mom's husband?" asked Selma.

"I tried," said Minnie. "Things are better, now." she said shaking off the bad feelings and smiling at Selma. "Tell me about Cendera."

"Well," said Selma thoughtfully. "Cendera is a place with strong magic. When my great grandfather and his brother came here from Italy, they happened upon the town. They had magic powers, and something about the town made their powers stronger. They settled there and made friends. They discovered the diamond mine when my great grandfather was looking for materials to make his mirrors. He made hand mirrors in Italy and he wanted to continue in this country. He discovered a special substance to make the mirrors from. While he was working on the mirrors, his brother discovered the emerald mine. When word spread about the mines, people tried to come in and take the jewels for themselves.

My great grandfather and his brother met with the leaders of Cendera. They worked up and cast a spell to make Cendera invisible to outsiders, and they made a barrier most people are unable to pass. They arranged for the only way in or out to be teleportation. They set out to make sure everyone in Cendera had everything they needed. The counsel was formed to handle all business. Today's counsel-members are descendants of the first counsel. Everything was going fine, until my great grandfather and his brother decided to take a trip back to Italy for a visit. While they were there his brother fell in love with an Italian woman. She did not want to leave Italy, so they came home to Cendera without her, but his brother was missing his love. He decided to return to Italy and make his home there. He took some diamonds and emeralds to start a new life in Italy. My great grandfather gave him three hand mirrors to take along. There were only six of the mirrors. They had been unable to find enough of the material to make more.

"The mirrors were magic. They did not know at first because they were men, but when women looked in the mirrors, sometimes they could see their true love. My great grandfather's brother took the three mirrors and sold them to a wealthy man in Italy. I heard that they were later sold to an antique dealer at an estate sale after the man's death."

"Wow," said Minnie. "I have read about the magic mirrors in the paper. I never dreamed I would meet a relative of the maker. I would love to have seen one."

"I will show you mine when we go home," said Selma.

"You have one?" asked Minnie gazing at Selma excitedly.

"Yes, my aunt gave me my mother's when I was fifteen. She has one, also. I don't know what happened to the last one. She explained about mine belonging to my mother and being made by my great grandfather and how he became an American citizen after he met and married my great grandmother. My aunt told me my father had tried to take my mother's mirror when he was leaving Cendera, but she had hidden it from him. He had to leave without the mirror. She even told me the mirror was supposed to be magic. She said it didn't work for her, but it had worked for one of her friends." Selma smiled at Minnie. "I knew Sal was my true love even before my guardian angel told me. I didn't know who he was, but I saw him in the mirror when I was fifteen. He wasn't looking at me, so he didn't see me, but I recognized him at once when he came to Cendera for the weddings."

"Oh my, what an amazing story," said Minnie. "Let's go find you a dress so we can go and see your mirror. I can't wait."

Selma laughed softly. "It's not going anywhere," she said as she rose and followed Minnie to the next dress shop in the mall.

When she followed Minnie into the next shop, Selma stopped in her tracks and gazed in amazement at the beautiful sea green dress she had been wearing in her dream.

Minnie looked at Selma and grinned. "I think we have a winner. Try it on and see if it fits."

"It will fit," assured Selma. "I dreamed about this dress last night. It's my dress."

Selma tried on the dress. It fit perfectly. After gathering shoes and a clutch purse to match the dress, Selma paid for the dress, shoes, and clutch holding them close in her arms as they made their way to Minnie's car.

When they arrived back at the Mase house, Selma excitedly modeled her outfit for Mrs. Mase and Minnie. They were very approving of the dress.

"You will be the prettiest girl at the dance. Sal will have to keep the other guys from stealing you away," remarked Minnie. Mrs. Mase smilingly agreed.

After taking the dress off and hanging it lovingly in her closet, Selma went to her dresser. She opened the bottom drawer and removed her mirror. It was wrapped in a shawl to protect it. Selma gently unwrapped the mirror and held it up for Minnie to see.

"Oh," whispered Minnie. "It's beautiful."

The mirror had a pearl like covering framing the round mirror and down the handle. The edge was framed in tiny emeralds. When she turned it to show the back, Minnie sighed in awe. The back was also pearl like, but it had a tree in the center. The tree had emerald leaves. In the dark substance, making up the trunk of the tree, the words TREE OF LIFE was written with small diamonds.

"This mirror is worth a fortune," said Minnie.

"It is worth more than a fortune to me," said Selma. "It is all I have of my mother's."

Minnie nodded her understanding.

"Would you like to look in it?" asked Selma holding it out to Minnie.

"Oh, yes," agreed Minnie carefully holding the mirror and looking in it. When she looked in the mirror, it started changing. Minnie looked on in amazement as Sandy appeared in the mirror. "Sandy," exclaimed Minnie.

Sandy had been washing his hands. At the sound of Minnie's voice, he looked up into the mirror. When he saw Minnie smiling at him, he looked behind him to see where she was. When he did not see her, he looked back at the mirror.

"Minnie, what's going on? Where are you?" he asked.

"I'm at your folks house. I'm looking in Selma's magic mirror," replied Minnie grinning at him.

"A magic mirror?" he asked.

"Yes, she brought it from Cendera with her," explained Minnie.

Sandy looked worried. "Does anyone else know about the mirror?" he asked.

Minnie looked at Selma. "Sandy wants to know if anyone else knows about the mirror?" she asked.

Selma shook her head. "No, I haven't shown it to anyone."

Minnie looked back at Sandy. "Selma said no. She has not told anyone about it."

Sandy sighed with relief. "Tell her not to tell anyone else. The last thing we need is for her to draw the attention of the witch hunters. I'll talk to Alex about it and see what he says," said Sandy.

"Okay, you know what this means, don't you?" asked Minnie.

"What?" asked Sandy looking puzzled.

"I saw you in the mirror. It means you are my true love," said Minnie grinning.

"I could have told you that," said Sandy smiling at her lovingly.

Minnie laughed. The mirror faded to its mirrored surface. Minnie smiled at her reflection and handed the mirror to Selma. Selma was smiling.

"I am glad the mirror worked for you. It only works when it wants to. You are lucky. I only saw Sal the one time before I met him. I would take the mirror out and look, but it never showed him again. Why didn't Sandy want me to show anyone the mirror?" asked Selma.

Minnie's face lost its smile. "He's worried the mirror might draw the attention of the witch hunters. He wants you to stay safe. He is going to talk to Alex about it. They have been working to stop the witch hunters. I think they have made some progress, but there is still danger."

Selma nodded. "I have been warned about the witch hunters. I will keep the mirror hidden. I would not want to put anyone in danger."

Selma rewrapped the mirror and stored it in the drawer.

"I need to be going. I have my homework to finish and supper to prepare. I loved our shopping trip. We will have to go shopping again soon," said Minnie as she gathered her jacket and prepared to leave.

"Thank you for taking me. I would still be looking without your help," said Selma. "I would love to go shopping with you again, soon."

Selma walked out with Minnie and waited while Minnie hugged and said goodbye to Mrs. Mase. As she closed the front door behind Minnie, Selma smiled with satisfaction. She was loving making friends in her new life. Selma straightened and turned toward the kitchen to help prepare the evening meal.

Mrs. Mase looked over at Selma when she entered the kitchen. "Did you girls have a good time?" she asked.

"Yes, we had a great time," said Selma smiling. "We went to the mall. It was fun. There is so much to do and see, all in one place. It was great. I will look forward to going again. Minnie said she had fun, too."

"I'm sure she did," agreed Mrs. Mase. "It's good for her to have a friend to hang out with."

"For me, too," agreed Selma. "The girls in Cendera did not want to hang out with me. They knew I did not have the vigilante powers. They also knew my dad had left me and did not want me." Selma looked up with a sad smile. "The funny thing is, they did not want to be around me because I did not have powers and my dad left because he thought I would have powers. He did not wait to see if I had powers, he just dumped me on my aunt and left."

"Did he try to get in touch with you later?" asked Mrs. Mase.

"No, after he left, I never heard anything else from him," said Selma.

"Would you like to try and find him?" asked Mrs. Mase.

Selma was shaking her head before Mrs. Mase finished her question.

"No, I don't want to look for him. I want to build a new life and go forward not backward," said Selma.

Mrs. Mase nodded thoughtfully and dropped the subject.

"I have everything cooking. It just needs keeping an eye on it. Why don't you go and do your homework? I'll call you when I need help," said Mrs. Mase.

"Okay," agreed Selma. She went to her room and opening her closet door, gazed at her lovely dress before going to her books and starting her homework.

After Minnie faded from the mirror, Sandy called the office to talk to Alex. He was answered by Brenda.

"Hi, Brenda, I was hoping to speak to Alex," said Sandy.

Brenda laughed softly. "Mariam had a doctor's checkup. Alex makes sure he is at each appointment. Mariam is over six months along in her pregnancy and Alex hasn't missed an appointment. Any time she tells him he doesn't have to go along, Alex reminds her it's his baby, too. He says he wants to be there every step of the way. I am sure Mariam likes having him along. She just knows how busy he is, but when he insists, she just smiles, kisses him and lets him come along."

Sandy laughed. "I can understand Alex's feelings. I'll call him later."

"Is there anything I can help you with?" asked Brenda.

"No, I just wanted to talk to Alex. I'll talk to him later. Thanks, Brenda," said Sandy.

"Okay," agreed Brenda.

After hanging up the phone, Sandy sighed thoughtfully. He then dialed Sal.

"Hello, Sandy," answered Sal.

"Are you busy?" asked Sandy.

"No, I am waiting for Alex and Mariam to get finished with her doctor's appointment. What's up?"

"I need to talk to you about Selma," said Sandy.

"Is she alright. Has something happened?" asked Sal anxiously.

"She's fine. There is nothing wrong. I just talked to Minnie. She and Selma had a shopping trip today. When they returned from shopping, Selma showed Minnie her magic mirror. I told Minnie to make sure Selma didn't show it to anyone else. I wanted to be sure she did not draw the attention of the witch hunters," concluded Sandy.

"I've read about magic mirrors in the paper. I had no idea Selma had one," said Sal.

"Well, she has one and it really works. Minnie was able to see and talk to me in it. I was washing my hands in the school bathroom. It startled me when I looked up at the sound of her voice and saw Minnie grinning at me in the mirror," said Sandy.

Sal laughed. "I bet," he said. "I'll be by after we take Alex and Mariam home."

"I'll see you then," agreed Sandy hanging up the phone.

Sal was still chuckling when Alex came from the building holding Mariam's hand. Micky came out first and held the door for them after looking around to be sure it was safe.

Sal held open the car door for Alex to help Mariam into the car. Alex looked at Sal before entering the car. "What's so funny?" asked Alex.

Sal shook his head. "I was just talking to Sandy. I'll tell you about it later. How's Mariam and the baby?" he asked.

"We are fine," answered Mariam. "Our son is going to be a gymnast. He's practicing his moves."

The men smiled and Alex squeezed her hand. "At least we know he is healthy," he said.

"Yes, we do," agreed Mariam smiling at Alex lovingly.

Micky and Sal entered the front of the car to start the trip back to the Avorn building.

Alex looked at Sal. "It's later. What did Sandy have to say?" he asked.

After Minnie and Selma went shopping for a prom dress, Selma showed Minnie a magic mirror she brought with her from Cendera," explained Sal.

"A magic mirror," exclaimed Mariam. "I read about them in the paper. I didn't know whether to believe it or not."

"According to Sandy, it is true. Minnie was able to see and talk to him in the mirror at school. He said she really startled him when he heard her voice in the mirror while he was washing his hands in the bathroom." said Sal chuckling again.

Micky and Alex grinned as they thought about Sandy's discomfort.

"Can we go by and see the mirror?" asked Mariam.

Alex looked at Mariam and squeezed her hand. He couldn't deny he anything when she looked at him so lovingly.

"Sal, call your mom and see if it is alright for us to stop by," said Alex.

Sal called his mom. "Hi, Mom, we are on our way home from Mariam's doctor's visit and she and Alex were wondering if it would be okay for them to stop and say hello to Selma."

Sal hung up and grinned at Alex and Mariam. "She said she will let Selma know to expect you," he said.

"You didn't mention the mirror," said Alex.

"I don't think Mom knows about the mirror. Sandy said he told Minnie and Selma not to let anyone know about it. He was afraid the witch hunters would hear about it," said Sal.

Mariam shivered. Alex drew her closer to his side. "Will we ever be free of those awful people?" she asked.

"We are working on it," said Alex softly kissing her lightly.

They were quiet as they drove to the Mase home.

CHAPTER 3

"*H*i, Mom," said Sal as he let himself, Micky, Alex and Mariam into the kitchen through the garage door. He went over and gave her a hug.

Mrs. Mase smiled at Alex and Mariam after Sal turned her to face them.

"It is nice to see you looking so well," said Mrs. Mase to Mariam She came over and gave Mariam a hug. She held out her hand to shake Alex's hand. "Is there something I can help you with?'

Alex smiled at her. "We were on our way back from Mariam's doctor appointment and Sal mentioned speaking to Sandy. He told us about Minnie and Selma shopping for a prom dress. Mariam wanted to come by and see the dress. Since we have not checked on Selma in a while, and I promised the council I would keep an eye on her, we decided to stop and see her and let Mariam see the dress.

Mrs. Mase smiled. "I will tell Selma. I have been busy in the kitchen, so I have not told her you were stopping by. Sal you and Micky wait in the living room. Selma would not want you to see her dress until prom night," instructed Mrs. Mase.

Sal and Micky, obediently, followed her instructions and went into the living room. Micky gave Sal a smile when he noticed Sal was uncomfortable with his mom's instructions. Sal scowled at him and promptly ignored him. Sal went over and turned on the television for them to watch while they waited. They settled on the sofa to watch the news show that was on.

Mrs. Mase led Alex and Mariam to Selma's room and knocked on the door.

Selma opened the door, prepared to help in the kitchen. She stopped in surprise when she saw Alex and Mariam standing there.

"Hello, Selma," said Mariam. "May we come in and talk to you for a few minutes. Sal told us you bought your prom dress. I would love to see it. Alex wanted to talk to you. He promised the council he would make sure you were happy here."

Selma stood back and held the door open for them to enter. "Please come in. You may tell the council I am very happy here. This is a wonderful place to live and the Mases make me feel like family."

Mrs. Mase smiled at Selma. "You are family," she said to Selma. "I have to check on my supper cooking. I will see you when you are ready to leave." She smiled at Mariam and Alex and left the room. Alex went over and quietly closed the door.

Selma looked at him in surprise. "You did not come to see my dress," she remarked.

"I do want to see your dress," said Mariam. "I also would like to see your magic mirror."

"How did you hear about my mirror? I promised Minnie I wouldn't show it to anyone," said Selma.

"Sandy told Sal about it and Sal told us," explained Mariam. "May I see it?"

Selma looked at Mariam's excited face and went to her dresser and removed the mirror from the drawer. She carefully unwrapped the mirror and brought it to Mariam.

Mariam accepted the mirror with an expression of amazement.

"It is beautiful," she said looking it over. "It would be amazing even if it wasn't magic." Minnie held it up so Alex could see it, also. Alex smiled. "It is very beautiful," Alex agreed.

Selma smiled. "It was my mother's. I treasure it because of her, but I love it for its beauty also, and because my great grandfather made it" she said smiling.

"Your great grandfather made it," exclaimed Mariam.

"Yes, he made all of the magic mirrors," said Selma.

Alex smiled as he saw the joy on Mariam's face. "He must have been a very special man. How does the mirror work?" he asked.

"It will sometimes show ladies their true loves," said Selma. "I saw Sal in it when I was fifteen. Their true love will only appear in the mirror if the person is in front of a reflective surface. Sal doesn't know I saw him. He wasn't looking at me. I didn't know who he was at the time."

"It is very lovely," said Mariam. She looked up at Alex and grinned. "Alex, go and stand in front of the dresser. I want to see if the mirror shows you."

Alex, obediently, walked over to the dresser and stood looking in the mirror. Mariam gave a gasp of surprise when Alex's reflection appeared in the hand mirror she was holding.

"I know you said it was possible, but to actually see Alex in the mirror." Mariam looked up at Selma and grinned.

"It does take you by surprise," agreed Selma.

Alex smiled at Mariam in the dresser mirror. "We have conformation of true love," he said.

"Yes, we do," agreed Mariam smiling back at him in the mirror she was holding. "It's a shame more girls can't look in the mirror."

Alex came to her side and put his arm around her. "When we are sure the witch hunters are taken care of, maybe Selma can work out a way for ladies to look in the mirror."

Mariam and Selma smiled at his words. Alex raised his hand. "I'm not promising anything. I said maybe."

Mariam grinned at him. "I know," she said. "You are my hero. I have gotten used to you performing miracles."

Alex laughed. "I'm glad I am your hero, but let's just wait and see what happens, okay?"

"Okay," agreed Mariam. Mariam reluctantly handed the mirror over to Selma, with a sigh, after one last look at it.

Selma wrapped it in the shawl and stored it in the drawer. "Could I see your dress, now?" asked Mariam.

"Sure," agreed Selma with a smile. She went to the closet and opened the door. The dress was hanging on the back of the door.

"Oh, it is beautiful. You are going to look amazing in it," Mariam declared.

"Thank you," said Selma flushing slightly. "I knew it was meant for me as soon as I saw it. I had dreamed about the dress last night."

"Wow," said Mariam.

"Maybe you have a different form of the vigilante power," said Alex.

Selma closed the closet and turned back to face Alex.

"I don't know about having vigilante power. I may have inherited some of my great grandfather's magic power." said Selma.

Alex smiled. "Maybe we can investigate your powers later. You need to keep them quiet for now."

"I will," said Selma with a smile. "I have kept quiet about my magic. I didn't want the council to know about it. They would have wanted me to stay in Cendera. I knew my destiny was not in Cendera."

"Did Minnie explain why you shouldn't let people know you have a magic mirror?" asked Alex.

Selma nodded. "Minnie said if the witch hunters found out about the mirror, they could target me or the Mase family."

Alex nodded. "We have been working to stop the witch hunters, but we do not know if we have stopped them all. I promised the council I would keep you safe. None of us want anything to happen to you or the Mase family."

"I understand," said Selma. "I will be careful about anyone finding out about the mirror."

"Good," said Alex.

"Thank you for showing it to me," said Mariam as Alex took her arm to guide her from the room.

Mariam pulled to a stop in the hall. She turned to face Selma. "Could I use your bathroom before we go?"

Selma smiled. "Of course," she replied. Selma showed Mariam the bathroom and then led Alex to the living room where Sal and Micky were waiting.

Sal looked up and grinned at Selma. She smiled back at him. Alex looked from Selma to Sal. Anyone would have to be blind not to see the attraction between these two, he thought.

"Did Mariam like the prom dress?" asked Sal.

"Yes," said Alex. "She loved it."

"What color is it?" asked Micky.

"It's sea green," said Selma. "The prom is on Friday, in two weeks."

Sal looked at Alex and grinned. "I need to be sure to have the night off on Friday in two weeks," he said as he smiled at Selma. "I'm going to be Selma's escort to the prom." Sal looked at Selma with satisfaction as he concluded his remarks.

Micky grinned, but, kept his attention on the television.

Alex smiled. "I'll keep it in mind," he agreed.

Selma flushed slightly. She was very happily looking forward to prom night.

Alex turned and put his arm around Mariam as she joined them. Mrs. Mase came in from the kitchen.

"Whatever you are cooking smells great," said Mariam.

"You are welcome to join us for supper," said Mrs. Mase.

"We would love to stay, but Alex has a teleconference scheduled. I promised him we would be back in time for him to take the call," said Mariam.

"I am sorry you can't stay. Would you like some chocolate cake to take with you?" asked Mrs. Mase.

"Oh, yes, that would be great," agreed Mariam.

"Make sure you have some for me and Micky," said Sal grinning at his mom.

"I already have some for you and Micky in a container," said Mrs. Mase. "You can come and get it while I fix Alex and Mariam's."

Sal, quickly rose and followed his mom into the kitchen.

Micky turned off the television and rose to escort Mariam and Alex to their car.

"We can go through the kitchen and collect your cake," said Micky. Micky was very comfortable in the Mase household. He was friends with both Sandy and Sal. He had spent a lot of time in the Mase household.

They collected their cake and said goodbye to Mrs. Mase. Sal squeezed Selma's hand and promised to be in touch soon. Selma hugged his words close as she bid them all goodnight. After they were gone, Selma started putting dishes out for supper.

Selma thought about the upcoming prom. It would be a great night. Sal would not be able to deny being attracted to her, and he would realize she had become a young lady. "His lady," thought Selma.

Sal and Micky were quiet and thoughtful as they drove Alex and Mariam to the Avorn building. They entered the parking garage and stopped in front of the private elevator.

Alex helped Mariam from the car. They were about to enter the elevator when Darrin and Becky exited the other elevator and called out to them. They stopped and waited for Darrin and Becky to come and join them.

"Hello," greeted Mariam giving Darrin and Becky a hug. "You must be getting off work." Mariam looked at Becky smiling.

"Yes," agreed Becky. "I am going to have to get me a car. It is too far for Taylor to give me a ride." Becky smiled up at Darrin. "I love having Darrin drop me off and pick me up, but it takes up a lot of his time."

"I don't mind," said Darrin. "I did want to talk to Sal and Micky." Darrin grinned at the guys. "You came by and picked the lots you want to build your houses on."

Micky and Sal nodded. "The architect is going to be at the building site on Thursday. I thought you might want to meet with him and give him your ideas about how you want your houses to be built," said Darrin.

Micky and Sal nodded. "What time Thursday?" asked Sal.

"He is expected around four," said Darrin.

Sal grinned. "I want to pick up Selma and bring her along. She should have a say in how my house is built," said Sal.

"You and Selma are together," said Becky grinning.

"Yes, our guardian angels said we are meant to be together," said Sal.

"That's great," said Becky gazing up at Darrin with a smile. He smiled back at her. They both had experience with listening to their guardian angels.

Darrin looked at Mariam. "How did your checkup go? Are you and the baby alright?" he asked.

"They are fine," said Alex hugging Mariam close to his side.

'Yes, we are fine. Our son is ready for the Olympics. He is getting lots of practice," said Mariam laughing up at Alex.

Darrin smiled along with them. "Have you decided on a name?" he asked. "The last time we talked you were still undecided."

Mariam gazed at Darrin seriously. "I wanted to ask you about the baby's name," she said.

Darrin looked at her startled.

"Alex and I want to name the baby James Alexander Avorn and call him Jimmy after our brother, if you don't mind," said Mariam.

Darrin looked at her smiling through moist eyes. He came over and hugged her. "I have no objection. I think it is a great idea. Jimmy would be honored."

Mariam turned to hug Alex when Darrin turned her loose.

Alex smiled at Darrin over Mariam's head. Darrin reached out and shook Alex's hand. "Thanks," said Darrin.

"It is what Mariam wants. I want her happy. I think Jimmy is a fine name for our son," agreed Alex.

Becky put an arm around Darrin and snuggled close to him. He smiled down at her and hugged her close. "We need to start for home. We have to stop at the grocery store on the way home," said Becky.

"Yes, we need to go. We will get together soon, Sis. Take care of yourself and Jimmy," said Darrin.

Mariam smiled through her moist eyes. "I will she promised as they watched Darrin and Becky climb into his truck to leave. Alex pushed the button to call their elevator. They told Micky and Sal goodnight and entered the elevator for their penthouse home.

After they were gone, Sal and Micky parked the limo and went to get Micky's car to head for their apartment. "I am looking forward to getting started on my house," said Sal. He looked over at Micky. "Have you thought about any changes in the plans for your house?" he asked.

"I think I will look at the plans and see if I find anything I want to change," said Micky. "We can go over basic designs and make changes to suit ourselves,"

Sal nodded in agreement. "I just know I want lots of room for kids," he said.

Micky glanced a Sal with a smile. "So, do I," he agreed.

They entered their apartment and headed for the kitchen. They were ready for desert. Other food could wait, but not Mrs. Mase's chocolate cake.

After eating and helping to clean up, Selma went to her room and removed her magic mirror from the bottom drawer of the dresser. She carefully unwrapped it and sat on the side of her bed to look in the mirror.

The mirror only showed her reflection. Selma sighed. "Why doesn't the mirror show me Sal," she wondered out loud. She sat there for several minutes gazing in the mirror. She was not paying any attention to the reflection. She was thinking about Sal and the prom. It was a good thing she had taken a dance class in Cendera. She hoped the dances here were not too different from what they were in Cendera. Selma sighed. "I'll just have to warn Sal not to expect too much from my dancing," she thought.

"I'm sure you will be fine," said Sal's voice from the mirror.

Selma looked in the mirror startled. She had not noticed the mirror changing and Sal appearing. "Hi," she said grinning. "I was not paying attention. I did not know I said that out loud," she whispered.

Sal smiled at her reflection. "I'm surprised we haven't seen each other in the mirror before," said Sal.

"I have seen you in the mirror before," admitted Selma. "You were not looking at me, and I did not know who you were."

Sal looked startled. "You must have seen me before you moved here," said Sal'

Selma nodded. "It was when my aunt gave me my mother's mirror. I was fifteen."

"Wow," said Sal. He smiled at Selma. "We have been meant for each other for a while. You were worried about the dance," said Sal. "All you have to do is follow my lead. I'll make sure you are alright. You will be dancing like a pro in no time."

"I'm glad we are going together. I would be embarrassed to admit to anyone else about how little experience I have dancing," admitted Selma.

"I'm glad you are going with me, also. Not just because of the dancing," said Sal seriously. "I don't trust those horny high school boys around my girl."

Selma laughed. She loved being called Sal's girl. "Those boys will take one look at you and they will know why I have not given any of them the time of day," admitted Selma.

Sal smiled. Micky came into view. He looked startled to see Sal standing in the hall talking in the mirror. "Are you talking to yourself?" he asked.

"No," said Sal with a grin. He winked at Selma. "I'm talking to Selma."

"Selma," said Micky looking in the mirror. "You can really see her. The magic mirror really works."

Selma laughed. "Tell Micky, yes the magic mirror really works," she said.

"You can see and hear Micky?" asked Sal.

"Yes, but he cannot see or hear me," replied Selma.

Sal laughed. "That's cool," he said.

"What's cool?" asked Micky.

"Selma can see and hear you, but only I can see and hear her," said Sal.

"Oh," replied Micky. "Goodnight, Selma. I will leave the two of you to talk."

"Tell Micky I said goodnight and thanks," replied Selma.

"Selma said goodnight and thanks," Sal told Micky.

Micky left with a wave and went to his room.

Sal smiled at Selma. Micky and I have an appointment on Thursday to look over our building plans for our new houses. I was wondering if you would like to come with us and see where we are building and look at the plans. After all, it is going to be your home, too," finished Sal.

"I would love to come along. I did not know you were planning to build a house," said Selma.

"It's going to be in Avorn Acres. When Alex gets finished with it. It will be an amazing place to live," said Sal. "I had better let you get some rest. I'll talk to you before Thursday. Sleep well and dream of me."

Selma smiled. "Good night," she whispered. The image in the mirror faded. Selma waited a minute to see if Sal's image returned. When the mirror stayed the same, she sighed and, rising from the bed, she wrapped the mirror in the shawl and placed it in the dresser drawer. Selma returned to the bed and lay back. She hugged herself tightly and smiled. "Sal is going to take me to see where his new house is being built," she whispered. She was almost too excited to think about sleeping. She closed her eyes and was soon dreaming about Sal.

CHAPTER 4

The next morning, as Selma was preparing to leave for school, she received a telephone call from her Aunt Phebe in Cendera. Selma was startled when the phone rang. She did not receive many calls. Selma had not heard from her aunt since she had called to let her know they had arrived safely.

"Hello, Aunt Phebe, how is everyone?" asked Selma.

"We are all okay. How do you like living in Oklahoma?" asked Phebe.

"I love it here. Everyone treats me very well, and I am getting ready to graduate from high school," said Selma.

"Have you applied for college?" asked Phebe.

"Yes, I am waiting to see if I am accepted," confirmed Selma.

Phebe paused. She acted as if she wanted to say something, but, did not quite know how.

"What is going on, Aunt Phebe?" asked Selma.

"Have you heard anything from your father?" asked Phebe.

Selma sighed. "No, why do you ask?"

"He called here asking about you. I was not home. He talked to Cecil. I do not know what all he asked, but Cecil told him where you were. Cecil said he asked about your hand mirror. Cecil told him he did not know anything about a mirror. You kept it covered to protect it, so Cecil had never seen it. He asked for your phone number, but Cecil did not know it," said Phebe.

"I wonder why he was looking for me after all of this time," said Selma.

"He probably needs money," said Phebe. "When he left, he took all of your mother's jewelry and all the diamonds and emeralds he could get his hands on. He also had access to the joint bank account he and your mother had set up. It had a good balance in it, but after your mother's death and your father left, no more money was added to it."

"So, he thinks I am his ticket to money," said Selma with a frown.

"That is what I think," agreed Phebe. "I may be wrong, but I do not think so."

"Well, you know him better than I do, so, I value your opinion," said Selma.

"Be careful. Do not let him sweet talk you out of your college fund. He can put on a good show when he is after something," warned Phebe.

"I'll be careful. Thanks for letting me know. Give the boys and Uncle Cameron my love," said Selma.

"I will. Take care of yourself. We love you," said Phebe.

They hung up and Selma sat on the side of her bed thinking for a moment. Then rising, Selma collected her books and went to the kitchen to talk to Mrs. Mase.

Mrs. Mase looked up and smiled when Selma entered the room. "Ready for school?" she asked.

Selma looked at her seriously. "Yes, but, before I go, I need to warn you about something," said Selma.

"What is it?" asked Mrs. Mase.

"I just received a call from my Aunt Phebe in Cendera. She said my father was trying to locate me. He talked to my cousin Cecil. Cecil is young and easily told my father whatever he asked. My father knows where I am and if he tries to come by here, don't let him in or tell him where I am," said Selma.

"Why is he looking for you?" asked Mrs. Mase.

"My aunt thinks he has run out of money. When he left Cendera, he took all the sellable items he could, but I'm sure they are gone by now. It has been twelve years," said Selma. "I'm glad I am over eighteen. He has no say in anything I do. When he left, he signed custody of me over to my aunt. It won't stop him from trying to get money from me."

Mrs. Mase shook her head. "It is so sad when a parent doesn't try to do his best for his child," she said.

Selma nodded. "I don't know if he is going to bother you. I just wanted you to be aware of the situation."

Mrs. Mase smiled. "Don't worry. I think you should let Sal know and have him tell Mr. Avorn. Mr. Avorn would want to know what is going on. He promised the council of Cendera he would keep an eye on you."

"I will, after school. I don't have time now. I have to go, or I will be late," said Selma.

"Okay," agreed Mrs. Mase. "I'll see you after school."

They said goodbye, and Selma hurried out to catch her bus to school. She was unaware of a car parked nearby. The person in the car was scrunched down. He was trying to not draw attention to himself as he watched the Mase house and Selma. He followed the bus until Selma exited the bus and entered the school. He then called a number on his phone.

"I found her," he said. "She is at school."

"Okay, is anyone at the place she lives?"

"There is an old lady there," he said.

"Maybe I should go and talk to the old lady."

"Don't do anything to draw attention or get us in trouble," he cautioned.

"I just want to reunite with my daughter. What is wrong with that?" asked Albert Dolan.

After Selma left for school, Mrs. Mase received a telephone call. "Hello." answered Mrs. Mase.

"Hello, Dora, this is Sally. I have been watching a car parked in front of my house for a couple of hours. There was a man in the car, but he just sat there and watched your house. He hid when Selma left for school. I was about to call the police when he started his car and followed Selma's bus. I don't know what is going on, but I thought you should know."

Mrs. Mase frowned. "Thanks for calling Sally. I don't know what is going on either. I will call Sal and see if he can help."

"Be safe, the people in this neighborhood depend on having you around," answered Sally.

Mrs. Mase smiled. "I plan on being here for my friends for a long time," promised Mrs. Mase. "Let me know if you see the car again."

"I will," promised Sally.

When Mrs. Mase hung up the phone, she was thoughtful. She thought about calling Alex Avorn, then, decided to call Sal instead.

"Hi, Mom, what's up?" asked Sal answering her call.

"I started to call Mr. Avorn, then I decided I would see what you suggested," answered Mrs. Mase.

Sal came to attention. "Has something happened?" he asked. Micky in the seat beside him looked over at Sal alertly.

"Selma received a call from her aunt in Cendera this morning. Her aunt warned her about her father snooping around, trying to find information on Selma. Selma told me to watch out for him," said Mrs. Mase.

"Maybe he was just checking on Selma, to see if she was alright," said Sal trying to reassure his mom and himself.

"Selma thinks he is probably wanting money, but that is not what I called about. After Selma left on the bus for school this morning, Sally down the street called and told me someone was watching the house and when Selma left on the bus, he followed the bus," concluded Mrs. Mase.

Sal frowned. "Selma is at school. She should be alright there until it is time to go home. Micky and I are on a case for Avorn. I'll call Alex and let him know what is going on. If Micky and I can't get over there, Alex will either send some other agents over to keep an eye on things or he may send someone to take over for us and let Micky and I come over. I'll let you know what he says. Try not to worry. Alex will take care of everything. I love you."

"I love you, too. I'll try not to worry," said Mrs. Mase as she hung up the phone.

"What's going on?" asked Micky when Sal hung up the phone.

"Someone is spying on Selma," said Sal. He quickly called Alex Avorn.

"Avorn," answered Lynn.

"Lynn, this is Sal. I need to talk to Alex."

"Just a minute, Sal," said Lynn as she put Sal on hold and punched Alex's number.

"Hello," said Alex.

"Sal is calling. He sounded stressed," said Lynn.

Alex smiled thinking how well Lynn could recognize their feelings. "Put him on," said Alex.

"Alex, Mom just called. She said a neighbor called and told her someone was watching our house. Whoever it was followed Selma's bus to school," said Sal.

"Does she have any idea who it was?" asked Alex.

"She thinks it may have something to do with a call Selma received from her aunt this morning. Selma's aunt told her to keep watch for her father. It seems he is snooping around. The aunt thinks he is after money," concluded Sal.

"I see," said Alex thoughtfully. "I will send James and Nelson over to check on her. Your mom knows James. She knows she can trust him."

"Good idea," said Sal.

"I'll make sure to send someone to take over for you and Micky by the time Selma is out of school. You can pick her up. I don't think it is a good idea for her to ride the bus home until we find out what is going on," said Alex.

"Thanks, Alex. I'll call Selma at lunch and let her know Micky and I will pick her up after school," said Sal with a sigh of relief, Sal turned to Micky and grinned. "Alex is going to send James and Nelson over to check on Mom. He is also going to send someone to take over for us so we can pick Selma up when school lets out."

Micky nodded. "I wonder why Selma's father decided to take an interest in her all of a sudden," said Micky thoughtfully.

"I don't know," responded Sal. "Maybe he just found out about her not being in Cendera anymore."

"I suppose," agreed Micky. "I hope your right."

"We will just have to wait and see," said Sal.

Meanwhile, Alex had called James and filled him in and asked him and Nelson to go by and check on the Mase household. Alex asked them to keep an eye on the place until Sal and Micky could take over. James was happy to obey his order. He had been meaning to go by and thank Mrs. Mase for helping his family. He had been busy and had not had a chance to go by and see her.

Mrs. Mase smiled delightedly when she opened the door to James' smiling face. "James," she said drawing him into a hug. "Is everything alright?" she asked drawing back.

"Everything is fine," James assured her. "Thanks to you and Sal. I have been wanting to come by and thank you and the church ladies. My wife is much better, and my kids are happier than I have seen them in ages. I also have thanked Sal for helping me get a job with Avorn. Your family has really made a difference in my family's life."

Mrs. Mase smiled and held the door for James and Nelson to enter.

"Mrs. Mase," said James. "This is Nelson Baker. He works for Avorn."

"Hello Ma'am," said Nelson nodding to Mrs. Mase.

"Hello, Mr. Baker," said Mrs. Mase before turning back to James. "Would you like some coffee?"

James nodded. "Thanks," he said as he and Nelson followed Mrs. Mase into the kitchen and took seats at the counter.

Mrs. Mase placed cups of coffee on the counter for them and placed the sugar bowl and creamer on the counter before them. She stood back and smiled to see how much they enjoyed her coffee. She had a special blend and she was very proud of how good it was.

"Did Mr. Avorn ask you to come by and check on me?" she asked.

James smiled, "Yes Ma'am. Sal called him and told him you had someone watching your house. Mr. Avorn wanted to be sure you were alright. He told us to make sure you were safe until Sal could take over. He said you are family and I pity anyone who threatens Alex Avorn's family. They don't know who they are dealing with if they try to hurt any of Alex's family," concluded James. He and Nelson exchanged grins of agreement.

Mrs. Mase smiled at the guys. "I have some sticky buns. I made them this morning. Would you like some?" she asked.

"Yes, Ma'am," said James and Nelson smiling and nodding excitedly in agreement.

Mrs. Mase chuckled at their enthusiasm and put buns on two plates and placed them in front of the guys.

Nelson groaned in pleasure. "Do you suppose we can get Alex to send us by here more often?" he asked James.

"It sure would be nice," agreed James savoring his sticky bun and washing it down with his coffee.

Mrs. Mase laughed as she watched the guys. "You guys are welcome anytime you want to come by," she said. "I really appreciate you worrying about me. When I received the call from Sally, this morning, I was frightened. Having you stop by has made me feel much better."

"Anytime you need help, you can call on us," Nelson assured her.

Mrs. Mase was offering them another cup of coffee when there was a knock at the door.

James and Nelson followed Mrs. Mase as she went to the door. She opened the door to see a stranger standing outside.

"Can I help you?" asked Mrs. Mase.

The man smiled winningly at Mrs. Mase. "I'm looking for my daughter, Selma. My name is Albert Dolan," said the man.

Mrs. Mase did not smile back at the man. "Selma is not here," she said and started to close the door.

"I know," said the man. "I would assume she is in school. I wonder if I might come in and talk to you for a minute and leave a note for Selma?" he asked.

Mrs. Mase shook her head. "I don't know you. I am not in the habit of allowing strangers in my home," she replied.

"I just want to leave a note," he insisted.

Mrs. Mase shook her head and moved to the side so he could see James and Nelson behind her. The man pulled back abruptly when he saw the two large Avorn Agents with Mrs. Mase.

"I'll check back later when Selma is around. Please, tell her I came by?" asked the man.

Mrs. Mase nodded and closed the door. She gave a relieved sigh. "I sure am glad Mr. Avorn sent you by," she said to James and Nelson.

"So are we," agreed James grimly. Nelson took out his phone and called Alex to let him know what was happening.

Alex had been expecting the news and he told them to stay put and promptly called Sal to fill him in.

"Have you talked to Selma?" asked Alex.

"Yes, I told her Micky and I would pick her up after school. I think I will wait until after we pick her up to tell her about her father's visit," concluded Sal.

"Whatever you think is best," agreed Alex.

Sal frowned as he hung up the phone after Alex's call. He thought about it for a minute, then decide to send Selma a text, "Your father showed up at the house. Everything is okay. Alex had sent agents over. Will pick you up at gym door. Sal." He sent the message off and looked at Micky.

"I thought you were going to wait," remarked Micky.

Sal shrugged. "I was, then I had a feeling. I felt she needed to know."

"Thanks for letting me know," said Selma's voice in his head.

"Wow, we can talk," exclaimed Sal startled.

"What are you talking about?" asked Micky.

Sal turned to him with a smile. "Selma talked to me in my head," he said.

"Wow," said Micky.

"Yeah, wow," said Sal.

"You can talk to me in your head, also. Close your eyes and think what you want to say," said Selma.

"I love you," thought Sal.

"I love you, too," thought Selma.

"I will see you later. I have to get back to work," thought Sal.

"I have to pay attention to my class," thought Selma.

Selma sighed. Sal said he loved her. Why was it easier to admit to love in their minds rather than in person. "He loves me. He really loves me," she thought. Selma tried to listen to the teacher, but it was hard. All she could think about was Sal. She could hardly wait for the class day to end.

Micky looked at Sal. He could tell Sal was communicating with Selma. Micky sighed. He was happy for his friend. He was impatient for his turn to come. It was easy for others to say be patient. It was hard to be patient when you want something so much. Micky sighed.

Sal grinned at him. "I never dreamed I could talk to someone in my mind," he said.

Micky smiled. "It must be amazing," he said.

"It is," agreed Sal.

CHAPTER 5

*A*lbert Dolan left the Mase house and drove to a nearby corner store. He stopped and joined his brother-in-law in his car.

"What did you find out?" asked Larry Scott.

"The old lady would not talk to me. She would not let me enter the house," admitted Albert.

"Why didn't you force your way in and find the mirror?" asked Larry.

"Because she had two large guys there with her. I didn't think I could get past them," said Albert.

Larry looked at Albert and frowned. "I don't know why I let Marie talk me into helping you find the mirror. There has got to be easier ways of getting cash," stated Larry.

"If Selma has the mirror, it is worth a fortune. I sold the one I brought with me from Cendera for $25,000. Selma's mother's mirror was worth more. I would have taken it, but I couldn't find it. I imagine Selma's aunt had it put away for Selma. I'm pretty sure Selma would not have left Cendera without it. If she doesn't have the mirror, she will have a healthy bank account. The council would have opened it for her when she left. Selma can be persuaded to help her dear old dad," concluded Albert with a chuckle.

Larry shook his head and sneered at Albert. "You are a piece of work," he declared. "How my sister fell for you is a mystery to me."

"Marie and I get along fine," declared Albert. She is also thinking about the boys. She thinks they deserve a share of what Selma is receiving."

"I'm sure you put the idea in her head. Couldn't you two teach the boys to study hard and work for their future. They shouldn't wait for someone else to make their future. They should be thinking about what they can do for themselves," said Larry.

"It doesn't hurt to have a little something to give them a start in life," declared Albert.

Larry shook his head. "The way you and Marie go through money, there will not be any left for the boys. They are only ten. Even if you get the mirror and sell it, the money will be long gone before the boys are old enough to use it," declared Larry.

Albert looked at Larry hard. "Are you backing out of helping me get the mirror?" he asked.

Larry paused and thought about what he was doing. He gazed at Albert. "I will not do anything to hurt anyone. I will help you keep watch, but anything else you can do for yourself. I am not going to jail for you or my sister."

Albert smiled. "No one is going to jail. I have a right to see my daughter. If she can be persuaded to help me out, that is not against the law," he declared.

Larry shook his head in disgust. He needed to stay away from his sister. He did not need to be persuaded into helping in her hairbrained schemes.

"What are you going to do now?" he asked Albert.

"I'll wait until Selma gets home from school and pay her a visit," stated Albert with satisfaction. He left Larry's car and returned to his. He may as well wait at home. It would be some time before

Selma was home from school. His boys were in school and Marie was home alone. It was the perfect place to pass the time.

~

Sal and Micky were waiting by the gym entrance, at the school, when Selma emerged. Sal exited the car and opened the back, car door for her when he saw her coming.

"Hi," said Selma smiling up at Sal.

"Hi," said Sal leaning down and giving her a soft kiss.

"Hi, Micky," said Selma when she was seated in the back seat and Sal was getting in the front next to Micky.

"Hi," said Micky smiling at Selma.

Selma looked at Sal. "What happened when my father went by the house. Is your mom alright?"

"Mom is fine. Alex sent a couple of guys by to check on her. They were there when your father stopped by. When he saw them, your father decided not to stay. What do you think your father wants?" asked Sal.

"I think he wants my magic mirror," Selma smiled. "He won't find it," said Selma.

Sal looked back at her. "How do you know he won't find it?" he asked curiously. "Where is it?"

"It is in my dresser drawer. It is wrapped in a shawl to protect it," said Selma with a smile.

Sal and Micky exchanged glances. "What am I missing? Why can't he find it?" asked Sal.

"Because it is invisible," said Selma with a chuckle.

"How can it be invisible?" asked Micky. "Mariam and Alex saw it."

"Yes, and Minnie saw it," agreed Sal.

Selma laughed. "They saw it because I unwrapped it and handed it to them. If they had looked in my drawer, they would not have been able to see the mirror or the shawl," said Selma.

"How did you make it invisible?" asked Sal.

"I used my great grandfather's spell. He made the whole of Cendera disappear. The mirror was easy compared to that," concluded Selma.

"Wow, imagine that," said Micky.

"Yeah, imagine," agreed Sal grinning at Selma.

"I haven't told anyone else about being able to cast some of my great grandfather's spells," explained Selma. "I did not want them to think I was weird."

"I don't think you are weird," said Sal. "I think you are awesome."

"So, do I," agreed Micky. "It is your secret. If you don't want us to tell anyone, we won't."

"Thanks," said Selma with a smile. "If the witch hunters found out, they would be sure to think I was a witch."

"They probably would," agreed Sal. "It will be better if they don't find out."

"Much better," agreed Micky.

They pulled into the Mase garage and went inside the back door. Selma followed Sal and Micky into the living room where James and Nelson were telling Mrs. Mase stories. Mrs. Mase was laughing at their latest story. They rose when Selma and the guys entered.

"Thanks for looking after my mom," said Sal shaking first James and then Nelson's hands.

"It was our pleasure," said Nelson. "Your mom is an awesome cook and she makes the best coffee I have ever had."

James looked over at Mrs. Mase. She was blushing slightly but smiling at them. "If you need us at any time, you have my number. You call. Okay," he said.

"Thanks, I appreciate you coming over. Tell Mr. Avorn thanks, too," said Mrs. Mase as she hugged James and Nelson and walked them to the door. Sal walked out on the porch with them to ask them about Selma's father's visit.

"What did you make of Selma's father?" asked Sal after his mom had turned and returned to the living room.

"He was very insistent until he saw James and me," answered Nelson.

"Yes," agreed James with a smile. "When he saw us, he couldn't leave fast enough."

Sal grinned. "I'm glad Alex sent you over to look after Mom."

"It was our pleasure. We don't like when our family is threatened," said James seriously.

"I think we are going to have to find out more about Albert Dolan," said Sal. He turned and looked as Micky opened the door and joined them on the porch.

"Where is Mom and Selma?" asked Sal.

Selma went to her room to do her homework. Your mom went to the kitchen to start supper," said Micky.

Sal nodded and turned back to James and Nelson to shake their hands and say goodbye. Sal and Micky watched as James and Nelson drove away. Sal glanced down the street and saw his mom's friend Sally on her porch. She waved at him and Sal waved back. Sal and Micky started walking toward Sally's house.

When they reached her house, Sally greeted them with a smile. Sal went forward and gave her a hug. "Thank you, Ma'am for looking out for my mom. I am so glad she has such a devoted friend in you," said Sal.

"We have to watch out for each other," said Sally. "There is a lot of mischief in the world today,"

"Yes, there is," agreed Sal. Micky nodded his head in agreement. "This is my partner, Micky Ansel. Micky, this lovely lady is mom's friend Sally."

Sally blushed slightly and slapped Sal on the arm. "It is nice to meet you Micky," she said.

"Ma'am," said Micky in agreement.

"We have to get back, but I wanted to ask you if you happened to get the tag number of the car you saw this morning?" asked Sal.

"Yes, I did. He just kept sitting there, so I wrote it down, just in case," confirmed Sally.

"Sally, you are an angel," said Sal giving her another hug.

Sally laughed and, reaching into her pocket, she pulled out a piece of paper and handed it to Sal.

Sal took the paper and looked at the number. "I'll need to have Brenda look up this number and see what she can find out," Sal said to Micky. "We have to go, but thanks again, Sally. If you need anything, call us. We are always there for you."

Sal and Micky turned to go, and Sally watched them for a minute before going inside,

"Such fine young men," Sally said softly to herself.

Sal called Brenda while walking home. He gave her the number, and she promised to look it up. When they entered the house, Sal and Micky headed to Selma's bedroom.

Selma opened her door at Sal's knock. She looked surprised to see Sal and Micky at her door, but she opened the door for them to enter.

"I was wondering if we could see your mirror," said Sal

Selma nodded and started to the dresser to take the mirror out.

"No," said Sal holding up his hand. Selma stopped and looked at him.

"I want to see if I can find it myself," he said.

Selma and Micky grinned at him. Selma stood back and pointed. "It is in the bottom drawer," she said.

Sal went over and opened the bottom dresser drawer. He looked down at all the lacy panties and bras in the drawer and grinned. He smiled at Selma and she flushed. Sal put his hand in the drawer and gently shifted the contents around.

"I don't see a mirror. Are you sure it is here?" he asked.

Selma smiled and nodded. She joined Sal at the dresser and reaching inside the drawer, she withdrew her hand holding the shawl and, unfolding it, she held the mirror up for them to see.

Sal took the mirror in his hand and held it up so he and Micky could see it.

"Wow," said Micky. "Are those stones real?"

Selma nodded. "Yes, they were mined in Cendera. My great

grandfather had access to all the emeralds and diamonds he needed. Everything he used to make the mirrors was found in Cendera. He also instilled them with his magic."

Sal and Micky were looking in the mirror. Only their reflections showed in the glass.

"It only works it's magic for women," said Selma. "I guess my great grandfather felt women should have a little extra help in finding their fated mates."

Micky looked disappointed, but Sal grinned. "I already know my fate," my guardian angel has been very vocal about Selma since we met in Cendera."

"My guardian angel has been dancing a happy dance since we met, also," agreed Selma with a smile.

Sal laughed and handed the mirror to Selma. "It is beautiful," he said.

"Yes, it is," agreed Micky.

"Thanks", said Selma as she wrapped the mirror in the shawl. She carried the mirror and, carefully, placed it in the drawer.

Sal and Micky watched her place the mirror in the drawer. When she started to close the drawer, Sal stopped her. He reached down and tried to find the mirror.

"I cannot find it. It has disappeared," he said.

"I told you it is safe," said Selma smiling.

"You must have some powerful magic," declared Micky. "Why did no one know about your magic?"

"I did not want them to know," said Selma.

"I am glad you trusted us," said Sal.

"Yeah," agreed Micky. "We won't tell anyone unless you tell us to," he agreed.

"Thanks, I know I can trust you," said Selma'

Sal pulled her close and kissed her lightly. "We had better go and let you get your homework done," said Sal.

Sal and Micky left, and Selma closed the door behind them. She closed her eyes and took a deep breath. Selma thought about how it made her feel for Sal to have his hand in her underwear drawer. It made her feel all hot inside just thinking about it. Selma sat down to do her homework. She did not know how she was supposed to concentrate on homework when all she wanted to do was be with Sal.

Sal and Micky went into the kitchen to talk to his mom.

"Something sure smells good," said Micky.

"Smells like tacos," said Sal.

Mrs. Mase looked at them and smiled. "James and Nelson were talking about getting tacos earlier. It made me hungry for them," she admitted. "I decided to make some. I haven't made any in a while."

"Your tacos smell better than any I have ever had," said Micky.

"No one can beat Mom's tacos," said Sal. "Sandy and I used to beg her to make them."

"Yes," said Mrs. Mase. "You boys would have lived on them if I had let you."

There was a knock at the door. "You stay here," said Sal. "Micky and I will see who it is."

Sal and Micky left the kitchen and made their way to the front door.

Sal opened the door and looked enquiringly at the man standing outside. "Can I help you?" he asked.

The man smiled. "I'm looking for my daughter, Selma. I'm Albert Dolan."

Sal looked at him hard. He did not say anything for a minute.

Selma had heard the knock at the door. She came to stand beside Sal.

"I'm Selma. Why are you here?" she asked.

"I'm your father. I heard you were here, and I wanted to see how you were doing. May I come in?" he asked.

Selma looked at Sal and nodded. Sal stepped back and let Albert Dolan enter. Selma led the way to the living room, and her father followed her. Micky and Sal were close behind him. Selma motioned for her father to take a seat. Sal sat beside her on the sofa and Micky sat in a chair where he could keep a close eye on Albert.

"Why did you decide to check on me after twelve years?" asked Selma.

"I thought you might like to get to know your family," said Albert.

"My family is in Cendera," said Selma.

"You also have two brothers," said Albert. "I'm sure they would like to meet you."

"I have two brothers," said Selma startled.

"Yes, they are twins. Bradley and Brandon. They are ten years old."

"I see," said Selma. She was quiet for a minute thinking. "You dumped me on my aunt, gave her custody, and wasted no time in starting a new family."

Albert flushed. "It wasn't like that. I had to leave Cendera. I was in no position to take care of a child on my own. I thought you would be better with your aunt."

Selma nodded. "I was. I should thank you for leaving me behind when you stole all of my mother's jewels and anything else you could sneak away with, including a hefty bank account," said Selma.

"It was a joint account. It belonged to both of us," declared Albert.

"I know," agreed Selma nodding.

"Did your aunt give you your Mother's mirror?" asked Albert.

Selma looked at him blankly. She had not expected him to come right out and ask about the mirror. Sal and Micky had tensed and were waiting to see what Selma wanted then to do.

"You took it. Didn't you?" asked Selma glaring at her father.

"Took what?" asked Albert.

"My aunt told me there was another mirror. She said it disappeared and no one knew what had happened to it. You took it." Selma looked at him sternly.

Albert started to deny taking the mirror, but after looking in Selma's face he stopped. "Alright, yes, I took the mirror. I sold it to help me get started here. I needed money to live on until I could get established."

"You had $30,000 in cash and several hundred thousand dollars in jewelry and uncut diamonds. How do you think you deserved my great grandfather's mirror?" demanded Selma.

Albert looked around at Sal and Micky. They were looking at him as if they couldn't believe what they were hearing.

"Do you want him to leave?" asked Sal softly. He gave Selma's hand a squeeze.

Selma looked at her father. I have nothing for you. I would like to meet my brothers and my stepmother. If you will leave your address and phone number, I will call and see when a good time to see them will be. I also want to know who you sold my great grandfather's mirror to."

"I will have to get back to you about the mirror. It was sold through Marie's antique store. I will have to check and see who bought it," said Albert.

Selma handed him a piece of paper and Albert wrote his address and phone number on it. When he started to hand it back to Selma, Sal took the paper.

"I'll give this to Alex Avorn. He will check and be sure you are telling the truth. He is Selma's guardian. He promised the council and Selma's aunt he would look out for her," said Sal.

Albert paled. He knew who Alex Avorn was. He knew he was someone he did not want after him. He rose to leave. "I will let Marie and the boys know you will be calling," he said.

Selma nodded and followed Micky and Sal as they escorted her father out the door.

After he was gone, Sal pulled Selma close in his arms. "Are you alright?" he asked.

"I'll be fine," said Selma laying her face against his chest. Selma pulled back and looked up at Sal. "I can't believe my own father stole one of my great grandfather's mirrors and was trying to get his hands on another one." Selma shook her head in disgust.

Mrs. Mase came into the room. "Who was at the door?" she asked.

"It was Selma's father," answered Sal. "He is gone for now. I'm going to give Alex his information so he can check him out. The more we know about him the better."

Selma nodded. "He was lying about a lot of what he said. He had some truth mixed in with the lies, so it was not easy to separate the truth from the lies."

"You can tell when someone is lying?" asked Micky.

"Yes. most of the time," agreed Selma.

"Wow," said Micky. "You are one lucky dude. I wish I could find me a lady like yours." Micky looked at Sal as he spoke. Sal grinned. "They broke the mold when Selma was created. There is no one else like her," he said and kissed her gently/

"I hear your dad coming in the garage door," said Mrs. Mase to Sal. "Let's eat." She led the way and they followed to the kitchen.

CHAPTER 6

*A*lbert Dolan drove to the antique store owned by his wife and her brother. He went inside to find Larry working stocking the store while watching the floor for customers.

Larry looked up when Albert joined him. He looked at Albert's stormy face and grinned. "I guess the reunion didn't go so well," he remarked.

Albert frowned at him. "It was a disaster. She had two bodyguards with her, and she accused me of stealing her great grandfather's mirror," said Albert.

"You did steal the mirror," reminded Larry.

Albert looked at him in disgust. "Yeah, but how did she know?"

"You said the people born in Cendera had powers. Maybe it is one of the powers. Maybe they know things," suggested Larry.

Albert shook his head. "My contact from Cendera told me that Selma did not have the vigilante powers," he said.

"Maybe your contact didn't know, or he was trying to put one over on you," said Larry.

Albert thought about it for a minute, then shook his head. "It doesn't matter. She knows and she wants to know who bought the mirror."

Larry frowned. "Marie is not going to like you giving out information on her customers. Especially the one who bought the mirror. She is a repeat customer, and she has been a loyal customer for years," said Larry.

"I know," agreed Albert. "I'll figure it out later. Right now, I have a bigger problem."

"What?" asked Larry.

"Alex Avorn is Selma's guardian and one of the men took my information to give to Avorn. He will have me investigated," concluded Albert.

Larry scowled. "You are going to bring Alex Avorn down on us," said Larry.

"What can he find? We haven't broken the law. All he will know is you and Marie own the antique store. We will look like an average family getting along as best we can," declared Albert.

"Maybe," agreed Larry. "I don't like the idea of being on Alex Avorn's radar."

"I don't like it either." Albert looked around. "Where is Marie?"

"She took the boys in for a dentist checkup," said Larry. Larry looked at Albert. "You know you could help out unpacking the stock," he suggested.

Albert frowned at him. "You seem to have it covered. I think I will head on home and wait for Marie and the boys."

Larry grinned as he watched Albert hurry out the door. "The best way to get rid of him is to suggest he work," observed Larry with a chuckle.

After eating and cleaning the kitchen, Sal, Micky, and Selma joined Mr. and Mrs. Mase in the living room. They settled down to watch television, but no one was paying much attention to the television.

Mrs. Mase was knitting. Mr. Mase had the newspaper. He was looking at the headlines. Sal and Selma were sitting on the sofa. Micky was sitting in a chair close to them. Selma was listening to Sal and Micky talk. Mrs. Mase would glance at them and smile as she concentrated on her knitting.

"Your father was not from Cendera. How did he and your mother get together?" Micky asked Selma.

"They met in college. They had not been dating long when he moved into her apartment, and when she became pregnant, they decided to get married. I was three years old when she graduated, and they decided to return to Cendera. My father did not hold a job for very long at a time. My mother was their main support. My mother was a writer. She did very well in sales. Her book sales were one reason they had a hefty bank balance when she died." Selma paused. She found everyone watching her and listening to her story.

"How did she die?" asked Mr. Mase.

"She saw a bicycle headed straight toward a one-year old baby. When she rushed to pull him out of harm's way, she managed to save to baby, but she fell and hit her head on the concrete sidewalk. She was killed instantly." Selma looked down as if fighting tears. Sal squeezed her hand.

"Your mother did a very brave thing," said Mrs. Mase. "I'm sure you are very proud of her."

Selma smiled at everyone. "Yes, I am," agreed Selma.

"Maybe Alex can find out what happened to your mother's things," said Sal.

Selma smiled and shook her head. "My guardian angel says not to worry. She said everything is as it should be. I don't know what she means," said Selma. "But I have learned to listen. If I am meant to have any of my mother's things returned to me, I am sure they will be."

Mrs. Mase smiled at Selma with satisfaction. "It is all in the Lord's hands," she said.

Selma nodded. "Yes, it is," she agreed.

Sal looked from his mom to Selma. He shook his head and glanced at Micky. Micky was grinning at him. He seemed amused by Sal's confusion. Sal frowned at him. Sal started to say something when his phone rang.

"Hello, Brenda," said Sal, after a glance at the screen.

"Hello, Sal, I have the name of the person, whose tag number you gave me. His name is Larry Scott. I did a search on him. He owns an antique store with his sister. Her name is Marie Dolan," said Brenda.

Sal looked at Selma. She was staring at him. "Married to Albert Dolan," said Sal.

"Yes, I went on and dug a little deeper when I realized she was married to Selma's father. They have twin boys. The boys are ten years old. They are in the fourth grade at school. They seemed to be well liked. Albert is supposed to help in the store. It seems he avoids working when he can. He spends most of his time hanging in the pool hall. He only goes to the antique store when he needs to mooch some cash from his wife. He invested in the store some years back. He had some jewels and cash. He seems to think the investment merits him a free ride. His wife is besotted with him and persuades her brother to tolerate him."

"The brother-in-law must do more than tolerate him. He was keeping an eye on our place and watching Selma," stated Sal.

"He just watched. He did not approach Selma," said Brenda.

"I know," agreed Sal. "Thanks for looking them up for me. Have you filled Alex in on what I told you?"

"Not yet, I thought I would give him a report in the morning. He was gone from the office, when I finished," said Brenda.

"Okay, I'll talk to Alex tomorrow," agreed Sal. "Thanks again. Good night."

They hung up and Sal looked up to see everyone watching him expectantly.

"Brenda says the man in the car was Larry Scott. His sister Marie is married to Albert. Larry and Marie own an antique store. It looks like Albert sold the mirror and jewels through the store. He is supposed to help around the store but spends most of his time in the pool hall. Brenda thinks Larry was just watching Selma for Albert. Probably as a favor to his sister. She did not think Larry was a threat to any of us," finished Sal.

"Did she say anything about my brothers?" asked Selma.

"She said the twins are ten and in the fourth grade. The intel Brenda gathered suggested the boys are good kids," said Sal.

Selma nodded. "I will have to meet them and see for myself," said Selma.

"We will," agreed Sal. "Micky and I will pick you up after school tomorrow. We are going to check the building plans for the houses we are having built. Darrin said we should look over the designs and see if we want any changes. When I told you about it, you said you would like to come along."

Selma was nodding. "I do want to go with you. I will meet you after school."

Sal took Selma's hand and pulled her to her feet as he and Micky rose in preparation of leaving. Selma walked to the door with them. They stopped to say goodnight to Mr. and Mrs. Mase. Micky said good night to Selma, and went to get the car, leaving Sal and Selma to say goodnight.

Sal pulled Selma close and kissed her gently. He leaned back and looked into her eyes. Selma smiled at him.

"If you have any trouble call me. Micky and I can be here in minutes," said Sal.

"I will." promised Selma. "Now I know what is going on, I will be fine. It was the not knowing that scared me."

Sal kissed her one more time and went to join Micky. Selma waved at them and they waved back. Sal lowered his window.

"Get inside," he instructed.

Selma shaking her head, went inside and locked the door.

"Inside and all locked up," she thought.

"Good," answered Sal's voice in her head. "I love you."

"I love you, too," thought Selma with a smile.

Selma said good night to the Mases and went to her room.

She took out her books and tried to concentrate on homework, but all she could think about was Sal. Selma smiled and shook her head. Sal was very bad for her concentration. She needed to think about her work before her grades started dropping.

"This close to graduation, I do not want my GPA to drop," said Selma quietly.

Sal and Micky arrived at their apartment. Sal went in first and went to the kitchen to get a drink. Micky lingered just inside the door. He was looking through the mail. He had brought the mail inside with him when he entered.

"Your true love is near," said his guardian angel in his head.

Micky looked up startled. He glanced in the hallway mirror. There was a girl looking at him. She looked just as surprised to see him as he was to see her.

Micky started grinning. "Hello," he said. "Who are you?"

"I'm Stacy. Who are you and how am I able to see you?" asked the girl.

"I'm Micky. Are you looking in Selma's magic mirror?" asked Micky.

Stacy looked confused. "Who is Selma? I'm looking in my mother's mirror. I don't know why I can see you," said Stacy.

"The mirror is magic," explained Micky. If a girl looks in the mirror, she will see her true love. Your mother must have bought the mirror from the antique store," concluded Micky.

"You mean you are my true love?" asked Stacy.

"Yes," answered Micky smiling.

"But I don't even know you," protested Stacy. Stacy looked behind her. "I have to go. My mother is coming. She mustn't see me with the mirror."

The girl faded from the mirror before Micky could say anything else.

Micky was standing frowning at the hall mirror when Sal came back in the room.

"What's wrong?" asked Sal.

"I just saw my true love in the mirror," said Micky.

"Great," exclaimed Sal. "Who is she?"

"All I know is her name is Stacy. She was looking in her mother's mirror. She had to leave quickly when she heard her mother coming. I don't think she knew the mirror was magic. She didn't want her mother to see her with the mirror." said Micky.

Sal shook his head. "Maybe she will get another chance to look in the mirror. If she does not get a chance at the mirror again, we know her mother bought the mirror through the antique store. If we find out who bought the mirror, we can find your girl."

"Yeah," agreed Micky brightening.

Sal led the way into the living room. "Your patience has paid off," commented Sal.

"Yeah," agreed Micky with a smile. "Just before I saw Stacy in the mirror, my guardian angel told me my true love was near."

Sal laughed. "Double confirmation," he said.

Micky grinned. "My wait is over. I get to meet my own true love," he sighed as he sat down on the sofa.

Sal sat down in a chair. He knew Micky was too excited to sleep. He was prepared to sit and keep him company while they both thought about the magic mirror and their own true loves.

Sal and Micky went into Avorn building and made their way to Alex's office. Lynn waved them in after letting Alex know they were there.

Alex looked up at them and leaned back in his chair and smiled at them. "Brenda forwarded me the report on Selma's father. Has anything else happened?"

Sal grinned. "Micky saw someone in our hall mirror last night," said Sal grinning/

Alex looked at Micky. "You don't look happy about it. Didn't you like who you saw?"

Micky shook his head. "It wasn't about liking her. I didn't get a chance to find out anything except her first name. Her name is Stacy.

She said she was looking in her mother's mirror. It may be the one Selma's father stole and sold at the antique store. Selma told us there were only six mirrors. Three were sold in Italy, Selma has one and her aunt has one. The only one left is the one her father stole."

"You may be right," agreed Alex. "I don't have anything pressing today. Why don't you two pay a visit to the antique store and talk to Marie Dolan. Maybe you can find who bought the mirror. You will be one step closer to finding Micky's girl."

Sal and Micky rose prepared to leave.

"Good hunting," said Alex.

"Thanks," answered Micky.

Sal and Micky waved at Lynn as they made their way to the elevator. She was talking on the phone and waved back without stopping to talk. Just as they were about to enter the elevator, Lynn called Sal's name. They turned to look at her inquiringly.

She motioned for them to return to her desk. Sal and Micky walked back over to Lynn's desk.

"Brenda wanted me to tell you that the person buying the mirror from the antique store was district attorney Mavis Clark," said Lynn.

Micky looked stunned. "Does she have any children?"

"She has a daughter in college and a son in the Navy," said Lynn.

"How could she have afforded the mirror?" asked Sal.

"She inherited a lot of money from her grandmother. She keeps a tight hold on her pocketbook. She spends on herself, but her children get little or no help from her. Stacy had scholarships to college and has a part time job to help with essentials," commented Lynn.

"How do you know so much about Stacy?" asked Sal.

"I went to school with her. We were friends. She is doing her student teaching at the local high school," said Lynn.

Micky was listening. He was stunned. His true love had been close, all this time.

"You had to wait for the right time," said his guardian angel.

Micky grinned. "I'm glad it is finally my time," he thought.

Sal turned to Micky. "Do we need to check out the antique store?" he asked.

"We should check with Alex," suggested Micky.

They went over and knocked on Alex's door.

"Come in," called Alex. He looked up surprised to see Sal and Micky returning.

"I thought you two would be halfway to the antique store by now," said Alex smiling.

"Brenda found out District attorney Mavis Clark was the person to buy the mirror," explained Sal. "We wanted to check with you and see if you still wanted us to go to the antique store."

Alex looked thoughtful. "I think we will wait and let them stew awhile. We will get to them later. Brenda is amazing. I believe she can find anything."

Sal and Micky nodded agreement.

Alex studied Micky for a minute. "I have met Mavis, and I met Stacy once. Mavis is one tough woman. She is a bulldog in the prosecutor's office. You are going to have to tread carefully around her. She rules her family with an iron fist," warned Alex.

Micky looked determined. "My guardian angel and the magic mirror say Stacy and I are meant to be together. No one is going to come between us," he stated determinedly.

Sal and Alex looked on smiling at Micky's expression of determination.

Alex handed Sal a paper. "Here is your assignment. You and Micky may as well have something to occupy your time. You can't do anything until school is out, so you need to keep busy. It will give you something to occupy your mind," said Alex.

Sal looked at the paper and grinned. Alex was sending them to the high school to check on some missing gym equipment.

Sal started out of the office and Micky followed. Sal turned and gave Alex a wave as he shut the door.

They waved at Lynn and headed to the elevator.

"What's our assignment?" asked Micky when they entered the elevator.

"We are going to be checking on some missing gym equipment at the high school," said Sal.

Micky grinned. "I love my job," he said.

Sal smilingly agreed.

CHAPTER 7

Sal and Micky parked in the high school parking lot and headed for the principal's office. The classes were changing, and the halls were full of students. Several of the students recognized Sal and Micky. They nodded or waved at them smiling. Sal and Micky helped with youth groups from the church. They were very well liked in the area. They greeted the boys with smiles and waves.

When they knocked on the door of the principal's office, they were instructed to enter.

"Hello, Principal Green, I'm Sal Mase and this is Micky Ansel. Alex Avorn sent us," said Sal.

Principal Green rose and offered his hand to first Sal and then Micky.

"Thank you for coming over. We didn't want to call the police if we can find out what is going on without them. Alex said he would send someone to check things out, but he said we may have to report it later. It will depend on what we discover. The staff will co-operate completely," concluded Principal Green.

"Could you tell us about what is missing?" asked Micky.

"It started out with small things. Everyone thought they were just misplaced. Then, it seemed to escalate. Someone went into the storeroom and took some boxing gloves. They were removed from the bottom of the box and the box was made to appear full. There are some missing helmets along with arm and leg padding. There are also some protective glasses missing," said Principal Green.

Sal looked at Micky and grinned. Micky smiled back at him and nodded.

"It sounds like you have someone wanting to be a boxer," said Sal.

Principal Green nodded. "I know. I have checked around school, but no one is talking to me about the missing items."

Sal looked thoughtful for a minute, then he looked at Principal Green. "Would your coach have any objection to Micky and I monitoring his gym classes for a few days?" asked Sal.

Principal Green smiled. "Coach Lewis will be glad to have you in his class. He is as baffled by the thefts as I am. He will be glad to know what is going on," said Mr. Green.

"We can't promise to find out who is taking things, but we will be better able to find out things if we can get the boys to trust us," said Micky. "We already know some of the boys, so it will help us to get answers."

"I appreciate Alex sending you over," said Principal Green.

"Alex always tries to help our young people," said Micky.

Principal Green nodded and rose. "If you will come with me, I will take you over to meet Coach Lewis."

They rose and followed Principal Green out the door and down the hall to the gym.

Principal Green knocked on a door to an office just outside the gym. He didn't wait for an answer, just opened the door and entered. The man in the office looked up and smiled at them.

"Hi," said the man. "You must be from Avorn Security."

"Coach Lewis, this is Sal Mase and Micky Ansel. Alex Avorn sent them to check on our missing items," said Principal Green.

66

"They would like to monitor your classes for a few days. They want to try and talk to the boys."

Coach Lewis was nodding. "I will be glad to have you," he agreed smiling. "I have heard about you two from some of my boys. They seemed to admire you greatly."

"I will leave you to talk," said Principal Green. "If you need me for anything, just let me know." The guys nodded, and Principal Green departed.

Sal and Micky looked back at Coach Lewis.

"We have a class starting. Come with me and I will introduce you to the boys," said Coach Lewis leading the way into the gym.

"This is a ninth- grade class. They are going to be playing basketball this period," said Coach.

When the boys saw them enter with Coach Lewis, two of them came over and greeted Sal and Micky. "Are you going to play basketball?" asked Simon.

Sal shook his head. "Micky and I will just watch you play. We didn't bring any tennis shoes with us."

"Okay, boys, since you already know our visitors, choose your teams," said Coach Lewis. "Lance and Gregory are team captains."

The boys lined up to choose their teams. Coach Lewis showed Sal and Micky to a bench where they could sit and watch the game. He went over to where they were choosing teams. He wanted to be sure the teams were chosen fairly.

The two teams gathered on the floor to practice. The boys not picked for the teams came over and joined Sal and Micky on the bench. Sal looked at Simon, who had not been chosen, and grinned.

"My parents yard looked really great when I was there yesterday," remarked Sal. Simon lived down the block from his parents. When Sal found out about Simon saving money for a bike, two years before, he had talked his mom into hiring Simon to cut their grass. Sal had even given her money to pay for the work. Simon did not know Sal was paying. Sal had asked his mom not to tell him.

Simon grinned. He was pleased with the praise from someone he looked up to. "Are you and Micky going to help at school?" asked Simon.

"No, we are here working on a case for Avorn Security," said Sal.

Micky looked at Sal startled. He did not know Sal was going to tell the boys why they were there.

Sal looked at the boys. "It seems the school has been missing some items. They asked us to see if we can find out what happened to the missing things," said Sal. The boys looked around at each other guiltily. Sal could see they knew what he was talking about. "Do you boys think you might be able to help us find the missing items?" asked Sal.

Simon hesitated. Another boy spoke up. "We did not want to cause any trouble. We were trying to help," he said.

"Help how?" asked Micky.

"We have a new boy in our class," said Simon. "He and his mom moved into our district after his dad died. His dad was a boxer He died when he was boxing. He was hit in the head while he had his helmet off. Joe wants to box like his dad. His mom won't let him because of what happened to his dad. So, we have been helping Joe fix up a place to practice in the garage at my house. My parents don't know about Joe's mom trying to keep him away from boxing. We just wanted to help him feel better about losing his dad."

"How could he spend so much time with you without his mom getting suspicious?" asked Micky.

"His mom is working as a waitress. She works long hours. The place they moved into is not in a good area. She likes having Joe over at my house while she is not there," said Simon.

"Who took the boxing equipment?" asked Micky.

"We all did," responded Simon. "Each one of us would take one thing until we had enough for Joe to practice with. He had his dad's punching bag. He hung it up in my garage."

Sal and Micky looked at each other and grinned. Sal shook his head. "You do know the items you have taken will have to be returned?" he asked.

All the boys looked despondent. "Are we going to be in trouble?" asked a boy.

"I don't know. I will have to talk to the principal and see," said Sal.

"Do you guys know the address of Joe's house?" asked Sal.

"Sure," said Simon. He repeated the address and Sal wrote it down.

The bell rang and the boys, after a quick goodbye, left for their next class.

Sal and Micky walked over and told Coach Lewis what was going on.

Coach Lewis shook his head. "I wish I could help. I hate to see Joe and his mom in such a bad neighborhood," he said.

"I'll talk to Brenda at Avorn and see if there is a way we can help. What do you want to do about the missing items?" asked Sal.

"We can't suspend the whole class," responded Coach Lewis grinning. "I'll talk to Principal Green. We can put a box inside the gym. I'll put a sign over it. It will say "All borrowed boxing items should be left here. We can get the school's equipment back and keep the boys out of trouble."

"Won't getting off so easy encourage them to do the same thing again?" asked Micky.

Coach Lewis shook his head. "Principal Green will give them a talk in assembly. He won't have to call out any names, but the boys will think twice about taking anything else,"

Sal nodded and looked at his watch. "It's lunch time. I guess we will take off," he said.

"Why don't you try our cafeteria?" asked Coach Lewis. "We have pretty good food there if you can stand the noise."

Sal and Micky nodded agreement and followed Coach Lewis to the cafeteria.

When Selma had taken her seat at a table in the cafeteria, Stacy Clark had stopped beside her table. "Could I share your table?" asked Stacy.

Selma looked at her in surprise. She had never met Stacy, but she had seen her around. Selma knew Stacy was a student teacher. "Sure," agreed Selma with a smile.

Stacy sat down and stared at her plate for a moment before glancing up at Selma. "Your name is Selma, isn't it?" she asked.

Selma nodded. Stacy flushed slightly. "My name is Stacy Clark."

"It's nice to meet you Stacy," said Selma.

"I know this is going to sound strange, but do you know someone named Micky?" asked Stacy.

"Yes Micky Ansel. Do you know Micky?" asked Selma.

"I saw him in my mom's mirror last night. He asked me if I was looking in Selma's magic mirror. I thought you might be able to tell me what is going on," concluded Stacy.

"Oh my," said Selma. "Your mom must have the third mirror."

"Does it really show your true love?" asked Stacy.

"Yes, it only works for women, and you should not tell anyone. The witch hunters will be after you if they find out. They will think you are a witch. I really can't talk about it here. We might be overheard."

"Okay," agreed Stacy wide eyed with wonder. "You can tell me about Micky."

Selma smiled. "Micky is a good guy. He works for Avorn Securities, and he is partners with Sal Mase. Sal is my guy," she stated firmly.

Stacy laughed. "I'm only interested in Micky. If the mirror and my guardian angel are right, we are meant to be together."

"If the mirror showed him to you, there is no question about it. You are meant for each other," said Selma firmly.

Stacy sighed. I never thought I would find anyone just for me," she said.

Selma looked up and grinned. "You are about to meet him without the mirror. He and Sal just walked into the cafeteria with Coach Lewis," she said.

Stacy looked around to where Selma was staring. Sal had already looked around and spotted Selma. He and Micky paid for their food and Sal led the way to Selma's table. Coach Lewis had gone to join Principal Green and fill him in on the missing items.

Micky had not seen Stacy's face until they reached the table. Sal sat beside Selma and Stacy looked up at Micky.

Micky stood there in shock. "Micky put your plate down before you drop it," said Sal.

Micky continued to stare at Stacy as he placed his plate on the table.

"Stacy," whispered Micky.

Stacy smiled at Micky and nodded her head. She reached up a hand to Micky. He took her hand and quickly let it go as they were both shocked.

"Sorry," said Micky.

"It's not your fault," said Selma. "It's the mirror. It will get better."

"The secret is to never let go, then you won't be shocked again," said Sal.

Stacy and Selma laughed.

"Are you going to sit down and join us?" teased Stacy.

"Oh, yes," agreed Micky sitting in the chair next to Stacy. He didn't start to eat. He was too busy staring at Stacy. "I can't believe I found you," said Micky.

"I'm glad you did. I was afraid I had dreamed the whole thing until I remembered you mentioning Selma. I decided to see if she knew what was going on," said Stacy.

"I haven't had time to tell her about your bad habits," teased Selma.

Micky looked at her startled. Selma and Sal laughed.

Stacy touched his hand. It didn't shock as much this time, so she didn't let go. "She said you were one of the good guys," said Stacy with a grin.

Micky relaxed and grinned at Selma. "Thanks," he said.

"I was only telling the truth," said Selma. Selma was trying to eat her lunch while holding Sal's hand and watching what was developing between Stacy and Micky.

"What are you guys doing at the school?" she asked Sal. "I thought you were going to pick me up after school."

"Alex asked us to check on something," said Sal.

Micky didn't say anything. He was too busy gazing at Stacy.

"Oh, they asked you to find the missing gym equipment," said Selma.

Stacy looked at her and they exchanged a smile.

"Yes." Sal looked at her seriously. "You know about it?"

"Everyone in school knows about it," said Stacy. "Are you going to be able to find the missing items?"

"We already did," said Micky joining the conversation.

"You did, that was quick," said Selma. "What is the school going to do about it?"

"They are going to let the boys return the items taken," said Micky.

"Oh," said Selma with a frown. "Poor Joe."

"You know about Joe?" asked Sal.

"Of course. We all felt sorry for him losing his dad and his home the way he did. I hope something can be done to help him," she said looking up at Sal pleadingly.

Sal shook his head. "You can stop looking at me like that. I already planned on talking to Brenda. I thought I could ask Darrin about it when we go to Avorn Acres after school." said Sal.

"Oh, if we weren't in school, I would kiss you," said Selma.

"Save it for later," encouraged Sal.

"Why don't you go with us after school," Micky said to Stacy. "We are going to be looking at house plans. I would like your opinion on my house. If you don't have anything else to do."

"I would love to go. I don't have anything else to do," said Stacy smiling at Micky and squeezing his hand, which she still held.

"Good," nodded Micky with satisfaction. "We can pick you up at the gym door after school."

"Okay," she looked at Selma. "you will be there?"

Selma nodded. "I usually ride the bus, but when I get a ride, we go to the back door to avoid the school traffic."

Stacy nodded, too. "I usually ride the bus also, but it will be nice to have a car ride for a change."

The bell rang and the girls quickly took their dishes and left them on the conveyor belt and, with a quick smile and wave, they left the cafeteria.

Sal and Micky stayed seated and Micky finally, managed to eat a little of his food.

Coach Lewis and Principal Green came by their table and stopped.

"Thank you for finding what was going on. I am glad I called Alex.," said Principal Green. "I will be sure and tell him what good agents he has," Principal Green smiled and offered his hand to each of them.

"We are glad we could help." said Sal. He looked at Principal steadily. "The boys had good intentions. They just need guidance."

"I know, I will try to make them understand there is a better way to do things," agreed Principal Green.

With a smile and a nod to them, he left. Coach Lewis stood by the table a moment longer.

"Are you two going to be monitoring any more classes?" he asked.

"We would like to come back some other time, but we have to report in today," said Sal.

"You will be welcome anytime you want to stop by. Next time bring your tennis shoes and join in," said Coach Lewis with a smile.

"We will. Thank you," said Sal smiling. He and Micky watched Coach Lewis leave before taking their trays over to the conveyor belt. They left the school well satisfied with their morning's work. They had solved the case. Sal managed to see Selma, and Micky had met his one true love, Stacy. It had been a very good day, and the day wasn't over.

Sal and Micky went to Brenda's office when they entered Avorn

Security Building. Sal gave her the address of Joe and his mom. They asked her to check them out and see if Avorn could help them. He explained about the dad dying and how hard a time they were having. Brenda took the information and promised to check on Joe and his mom.

Brenda smiled at Sal and Micky and shook her head. "You do know we have a waiting list for housing in Avorn Acres."

Micky nodded. "We know, but some cases are more urgent than others. This boy needs help. He is dealing with the loss of his dad. He doesn't need gang members trying to recruit him."

Brenda nodded her agreement. "I'll check on them. Maybe we can help them," she said.

"Thanks, Brenda," said Sal and Micky as they left her office and headed for Alex's office.

Alex looked up with a smile when they entered. "Well, did you find Stacy?" he asked Micky.

Micky grinned. "Don't you want to know how the job went?" he asked.

"I already know about the job. Principal Green called me. He said my agents were amazing. They solved the case in record time. I agreed with him. I want to know about Stacy," said Alex with a grin.

"We had lunch with Stacy and Selma," said Sal. "They are going with us after school to look at the designs for our new houses."

"Good," said Alex with satisfaction. "I figured if I put you in the same area as Stacy, your guardian angel would take over and bring you together."

Micky smiled. "Thanks, Alex.

"You're welcome. Now you guys get out of here and go pick up your girls." said Alex.

Sal and Micky started to leave, when Sal looked back at Alex. "Will it be alright if we arrange boxing lessons in Avorn gym for Joe? He is the boy the students were trying to help. His dad died and Joe is having a hard time recovering from his death," explained Sal.

Alex nodded. Go by the gym and tell them to issue a lifetime membership in Avorn gym. Have it to include a pass for a companion when he visits the gym. Tell them it is to state it is for Joe Sills in honor of his father Arnold Sills. I should have thought of it before. Arnold Sills was a great boxer, and feather weight champion for several years. He deserves to be honored. I am going to see about hanging a plaque in the gym honoring him."

Sal and Micky were smiling. They were well pleased with Alex's response.

CHAPTER 8

Sal and Micky headed back to the school after stopping by the gym and getting a gym membership for Joe. They went to Principal Green's office.

Principal Green looked up and smiled when Sal and Micky entered his office. "I didn't expect to see you guys back here today," he said.

"We have something we wanted you to pass on to Joe in assembly," said Sal.

Sal handed him the card showing Joe's lifetime membership in Avorn gym.

Principal Green looked at it in surprise. "This is very generous of Alex," he stated.

Sal and Micky just smiled. "Alex said to be sure Joe knows he can bring a companion with him when he goes to the gym. Also, he wants Joe to know Avorn Gym is going to be putting a plaque on their wall honoring his father as a featherweight champion of the world. There will be a ceremony when it is hung and Joe and his mom will be invited to attend," said Micky.

Principal Green stood and smiled at the guys. "I will be sure the boys all know about the gym pass and the plaque. All the boys, not just Joe, deserve to know their efforts are not wasted and there are people who care and will help. Thank you for all of your help." Principal Green held out his hand and shook first Sal and then Micky's hands.

Sal and Micky left and went outside to get their car. They drove around to the gym entrance to pick up Selma and Stacy. The girls were just coming out the door when they pulled up to the entrance. Micky jumped out and quickly opened the back door for them. He and Stacy smiled at each other as the girls said hello and seated themselves. They put on their seat belts. Sal greeted Selma as Micky took his seat in the front.

"I'm glad you will be able to see my designs," Micky looked back to speak to Stacy. "I want you to tell me if there is anything you don't like. I want you to be happy with our home."

"You are getting a little ahead of yourself. We just met," said Stacy.

Micky nodded. "I know, but the mirror and my guardian angel told me we are true loves. It will take a while to build the house. I want to be sure you like it before I start building," concluded Micky.

"Okay," agreed Stacy. She glanced over at Selma. "Are you and Sal engaged?"

"No, we have to wait awhile before we can be engaged or married. I must graduate and start college. I will also have to make arrangements for my aunt and her family to attend the wedding," said Selma.

"What?" asked Sal startled. "I didn't know you were going to want them to come from Cendera for our wedding. I hoped we were going to have a small ceremony at our church."

"We can have a small wedding at the church, when you ask me to marry you, but I still want my family to come," said Selma.

Sal looked at her in the rear view mirror and groaned. "I'll have to talk to Alex when the time comes and see if he can arrange for them to visit," he said.

Selma grinned at his reflection in the mirror. "Thanks," she said.

"Where is Cendera?" asked Stacy'

"It is the town where I grew up. It is hard to explain. I'll tell you about it later," said Selma as Sal pulled into the gate of Avorn Acres. The guard waved them through, and Sal was soon pulling to a stop in front of the office building.

They went inside and saw Darrin talking to two men. They had house designs open on the table. They were studying them and discussing changes.

Darrin looked up when they entered and came toward them smiling. He offered his hand to Sal and Micky. He said hello to Selma and looked at Stacy enquiringly.

"This is Stacy Clark. She is with me," said Micky putting an arm around Stacy.

"It's nice to meet you Stacy," said Darrin grinning.

"Stacy, this is Darrin Semp. He is the building manager for Avorn Acres and Alex's brother-in-law," said Micky.

"It's nice to meet you, Darrin," said Stacy.

"We came by to check our house plans," said Sal.

"Jim and Hal were showing me the plans. You both picked similar house designs. There are a few differences, but not many," said Darrin leading the way to the table where the plans were spread.

After greeting Jim and Hal, Sal and Micky, holding tight to Selma and Stacy's hands, leaned over the table and studied the plans.

Darrin smiled. He could see Selma and Stacy were having trouble understanding the plans. "We have two tables. Sal, why don't you take your plans to the other table. You and Selma can study them better over there and it will make it easier for Micky and Stacy to study his plans at this table?"

Hal gathered Sal's plans and carried them to the other table. He spread them out for Sal and Selma to look over. Sal seated Selma and took a chair beside her. Micky seated Stacy at their table and sat beside her to explain his house plans to her.

"This looks like a large house," said Selma.

"It's not so large. It is only four bedrooms," said Sal. He grinned at Selma. "We need to be sure we will have plenty of room for future generations," stated Sal softly.

Selma looked at him startled. "Let's take care of this generation before worrying about future ones," she said.

Sal smiled. He turned his attention to the plans. After studying them for a few minutes, he sat back and smiled. "These look pretty good to me. I just would like a large screened in porch added to the back. The basement will be perfect for a storm shelter. Everything else looks like what we discussed before. Do you see anything you would like different?" he asked Selma.

Selma hesitated. "What is it?" asked Sal.

"I think the pantry should be larger, so you can walk in it, and it should have shelves down the walls," said Selma.

Sal looked at where she was pointing. He turned to Hal, who was watching them. "Can the pantry be changed?" he asked.

"Sure," said Hal. "I already made a note of it. I also made a note about your screened in porch."

"I would also like the attic made into a large room with insulation and walls. It can be used as a playroom or converted to bedrooms as needed," said Sal.

Hal made a note of Sal's comments.

"Do you see anything else you want changed?" Sal asked Selma. She shook her head. "I guess we are done," he said. "Thanks, Hal. If Micky and Stacy are finished, we can show you girls where the houses are going to be built."

He held Selma's hand and led the way to where Micky and Stacy were finished going over their plans.

Darrin came over and met them as they were getting ready to leave. "If you think of anything else you want to change, let me know. We will be starting construction in about a week."

Sal and Micky nodded in agreement. "We will," they agreed.

Once outside, Micky helped Stacy into the front passenger seat and seated himself in the driver's seat. Sal helped Selma into the back seat and circling the car took the other back seat beside her. When Sal entered the car, he reached for Selma's hand and pulled her as close as he could get with the seat belt on.

Micky smiled at Stacy and started the car to drive to the other side of the subdivision.

Micky stopped the car in front of two empty lots. There was a children's playground on one side. The other side had a house foundation started on it. There was a fence between the playground and the first lot.

Micky and Sal exited the car and helped the girls out. They stood looking around. Sal and Micky anxiously watched the girls to see their reaction to the location.

"The lots are extra- large", said Micky.

"Yes," agreed Sal. "They are a half acre. Most lots are one fourth acre."

Selma smiled and reached for Sal's hand. "It is a beautiful location. We will have a great view of the hills from our screened-in porch." She leaned in and kissed his cheek. Sal turned and kissed her mouth.

Stacy, seeing how anxious Micky looked, smiled also. "I agree with Selma. I'm glad we decided to add a screened-in porch. It seems we all think alike," she said.

Micky relaxed with a grin and squeezed her hand. "I am so glad you are with me today. I have been waiting for you forever."

He pulled her close and placed a gentle kiss on her lips. Stacy started to tense, then relaxed and returned his kiss.

Selma pulled back and smiled at Sal. "It sounds like Micky had the same idea as you did about the screened- in back porch," said Selma.

Sal pulled her close and kissed her again. When he stopped kissing and started looking around again, he grinned. "Micky and I were talking about the porch a few days ago. I knew I wanted one, but I wasn't sure he was going to have one added. He was undecided the last time we talked. I guess Stacy helped him make up his mind."

"It will definitely be a place to enjoy on summer days," added Selma. "We will have to hang a shade between our place and theirs so we can really enjoy the porch," said Selma.

Sal leaned back and grinned at her. "I like the way you think," he remarked. "Would you girls like to go out to eat?" asked Sal loud enough for Stacy to hear.

"I would love to," said Selma.

"So, would I," agreed Stacy.

"You need to call your mom and let her know we won't be home. She needs to know before she starts preparing her evening meal," said Selma.

Sal nodded and took out his phone to call his mom.

He hung up after talking with his mom. "Mom says for us to enjoy ourselves," said Sal.

"We will," said Micky gazing at Stacy.

Sal took the driver's seat this time, with Selma in front with him. Micky helped Stacy into the back seat beside him. Sal headed the car for the back entrance to the subdivision. He pulled to a stop as the guard came out and held up his hand to stop the car.

"Hi, Leo, how are things going?" asked Sal after rolling down his window.

Leo smiled at Sal and Micky and flashed a curious look at the girls with them.

"Everything is going great, Sal. My family is happy I decided to take Alex up on his offer of gate duty. My wife thought I was getting too old for street duty. She loves the house Alex gave us with the job. Are you and Micky here checking on your houses?"

"Yes, we wanted to show our ladies our house plans," said Sal. "Leo this is my lady, Selma and Micky's lady is Stacy."

"It's nice to meet you, Ladies," said Leo.

Both girls smiled and greeted Leo.

"I wanted you to meet them, so you can look out for them if they come here without Micky or myself," said Sal.

"Are there many guards in Avorn Acres, Leo?" asked Selma.

"We have six gate guards," said Leo. "There are three gates, and each guard works eight hours on and eight hours off. We rotate which gate we are at, so the guards are familiar with everyone who goes in and out of the subdivision. We also have two guards patrolling the streets. They make sure there is no trouble and fill in for the gate guards if one is sick or has an emergency."

"Wow," said Stacy. "Mr. Avorn is sure into safety."

"Yes," agreed Leo. "Alex wants the people here to be as safe as he can make them."

Leo looked at Sal. "The people here in Avorn Acres want to do something to honor Alex and let him know how much they appreciate all he is doing for them."

Sal was shaking his head. "Alex wouldn't want them to do anything like that," said Sal.

Leo nodded. "We know. So, we had another idea. We want to put a statue in the park. It is at the center of the subdivision and has benches for people to sit and enjoy the outdoors."

"What kind of statue?" asked Micky.

Leo glanced at Micky. "A statue of an angel. There would be a plaque on the bottom honoring the Semp family. An angel would be above the plaque with its hands upraised holding a heart. In the heart would be the words. "Flying High". We thought Alex could not turn down a statue honoring Mariam's family."

"That is beautiful," sniffed Selma with misty eyes.

"Yes, it is," agreed Stacy blinking her eyes.

Sal and Micky grinned at Leo. "You have Alex pegged. There is no way he could deny having a statue for Mariam's family. He will really appreciate the honor. You guys could not have come up with anything Alex would like more," concluded Sal.

"It doesn't hurt to stay on the good side of your building manager, either," said Micky.

"We thought so, too," agreed Leo grinning. "You think it is a good idea?" asked Leo.

"I think it is a great idea," agreed Sal.

"I'll tell our group to go forward. Please don't tell Alex, yet. We would like to surprise him if we can," said Leo.

"We won't say a word. When you tell him will be up to your people. If there is anything we can do to help let us know. After all, we are going to be residents of Avorn Acres as soon as our houses are built," said Sal. Micky nodded agreement.

Leo smiled and agreed. "Thanks Sal. I'll tell everyone. You guys have a nice evening. It was nice to meet your ladies. We will watch out for them and keep them safe when they are here," he promised Sal and Micky.

"Thanks, Leo." Sal waved his hand and drove through the gate. Leo closed the gate and went inside his gate house. He started calling around. He was spreading the word to go forward with the statue. When he hung up his phone, Leo sat back with a sigh of satisfaction. Alex did so much for everyone in need. It was time for the people, he had helped, to give a little back.

Sal drove to a restaurant he and Micky were familiar with. They had good food. The people were friendly, and they could be sure to enter with-out a reservation."

"Holiday's," said Selma reading the sign.

"Have you been here before?" Micky asked Stacy.

"I was here once with my brother. He brought me here before he shipped out. It has good food. Although I didn't do the food justice. I was so sad my brother was leaving," said Stacy.

Micky squeezed her hand. "I'm sorry you were sad. Maybe we can give you some better memories of the place."

Stacy smiled and squeezed his hand also.

The guys helped the ladies out of the car and, with their arms around their shoulders, led them into Holiday's. They were greeted with big smiles and taken to a semi- private booth. Sal stood back and let Selma be seated on one side, then sat down beside her. Micky and Stacy were seated on the other side.

The waitress brought them water and menus. "Welcome to Holiday's. What can I get for you?" she asked.

Sal smiled. "Which holiday are we celebrating today?" he asked.

The waitress smiled back "We are celebrating an Irish holiday. The cook made a big pot of Mulligans Stew," she said.

Sal handed her back his menu. "I want the stew and iced tea," he said.

"The stew is well seasoned," warned the waitress.

Sal grinned. "I know. I have had it before," he smiled.

Selma and Stacy, looking dubious, decided to try the stew. Micky grinned and added his order of stew.

The waitress smiled and took their menus. She promised their food would be right out and left a pitcher of tea on the table for refills. She knew a large amount of tea would be needed with the stew.

"How hot is this stew?" asked Selma.

"It is not so bad. It just takes a little getting used to," said Sal with a grin.

Micky hid a smile as Stacy looked at him. Stacy and Selma exchanged a look and shrugged. They would soon find out.

The waitress brought their bowls of stew. She placed a bowl before each of them and placed a platter of cornbread in the center of the table. "If you need anything else, let me know," said the waitress.

Sal and Micky took up their spoons and ate a bite of stew. Selma and Stacy closely watched them. When neither flinched, the girls took their spoons and ate a small bite of the stew.

"Oh, my," exclaimed both girls reaching for their tea. After a long drink, Selma looked at Sal. "My mouth is on fire," she whispered. Stacy nodded her agreement and drank some more tea.

"It will get better after you eat some more," encouraged Sal. "The first bite is always the hottest."

Micky looked at Stacy like he didn't know what to say. "Are you alright?" he asked.

Stacy smiled at him. "I will be fine. It caught me by surprise. I like spicy food. I just wasn't expecting it to be so hot," she said.

"It will get better," said Micky. "Try some more."

Selma and Stacy raised their spoons and ate another small bite. They both looked surprised when it didn't burn as bad this time.

"Try some corn bread with it," encouraged Sal. He handed Selma a piece of corn bread and took one for himself. Micky reached for two pieces of bread and passed one to Stacy.

The girls nibbled the bread and ate another bite of the stew. They found the cornbread helped and were soon eating larger bites. Sal and Micky finished their bowls and held them up for refills. The waitress brought them fresh bowls and carried their old bowls away.

Selma glanced at Sal and Micky digging into fresh bowls and at her half-eaten bowl of stew. "You guys must have cast iron stomachs," she remarked.

Sal and Micky smiled. "We eat here whenever we can," said Sal. "We are used to the spicy food. Holiday's celebrates holidays all over the world. Most other countries put a lot more spices in their food than we do in our country."

"I have heard some of my classmates at college talking about the bland taste of American food," said Stacy. "One of my favorite foods is Mexican chili."

Micky grinned. "I love Mexican chili," he remarked.

They concentrated on finishing their food. When the waitress offered them desert, they all refused. "It was good, but I couldn't eat another bite," said Selma. Stacy agreed. Sal and Micky put some money on the table for the food and the tip and led the girls to the door.

They emerged into a warm, breezy evening.

"Do you girls have to go home, or would you like to go for a drive?" asked Sal.

"I would love to go for a drive," said Stacy.

"So. would I," agreed Selma. "I can do my homework later. I don't have very much homework. The teachers are taking it easy on us, because we are preparing for prom and studying for finals."

Stacy sighed. "I was roped into attending the prom," she said. "They need teachers to keep an eye on things."

"Do you need a date?" asked Micky with a grin.'

"Are you offering?" asked Stacy.

"I would love to be your date," said Micky.

"I would love for you to be my date," said Stacy.

Micky drew her close and kissed her lightly.

Selma grinned at Sal with happiness. She was going to have friends with her in this new life. She was really looking forward to her prom and her date with Sal. Sal grinned at Selma. He was looking forward to prom night, Having Micky and Stacy along made it even better.

CHAPTER 9

S al drove toward the edge of town, where there were less streetlights. They would be able to see the stars better in a short while. It was almost evening and the moon was rising. As they drove down one street, Selma sat forward in surprise.

"Oh, look, there is a fair over there," she said pointing at the lights and the sound of music.

The others looked the way she was pointing. Stacy smiled wistfully. "I haven't been to a street fair in years," she said.

"Would you like to stop?" asked Micky.

Stacy looked at Micky with a huge grin. "Could we?" she asked.

Micky looked at Sal. "We don't have to check in with Alex. We could stop for a while to check it out," he said.

Sal looked at Selma's wistful expression and turned to the street hosting the fair.

Selma was so happy. She was practically bouncing in her seat.

After Sal found a parking place, he hurried around the car to open Selma's door before she could open it herself. He took her hand and help her to stand. Selma stood staring around in wonder. They never had events like this in Cendera.

"It is great," she said. "I hardly know where to look first."

"Why don't we wander around and see what the fair has to offer," said Sal taking her hand and slowly leading her forward.

"Have you been to a fair before?" asked Sal.

Selma shook her head. "I don't remember them ever having a fair in Cendera," she said.

Stacy, overhearing her remark, looked at Selma startled. "Your town never had a street fair?" she asked.

Selma shook her head. "I guess the council never thought of it. Maybe no one asked for one." Selma shrugged. If it had been requested, they would have arranged for one. They tried to meet most requests."

Stacy stared at Selma. "I have never heard of a town like the one you came from," she stated.

"Not many have," agreed Selma.

Sal and Micky decided it was time to change the subject. Micky drew the girl's attention to a shooting booth. It had stuffed toys as prizes. "Would you like me to win you a stuffed toy?" Micky asked Stacy.

Stacy looked at him with shining eyes. "No one has ever won a prize for me. Do you think you can?" she asked.

"I can try. Alex makes sure we are up to date with our target practice," he said.

They walked over to the booth. Micky paid for three tries and the boy in the booth handed him a gun. Micky handled the gun to see how it felt in his hand. After checking the gun out, Micky carefully aimed at the target. He hit the edge of the center mark.

"It pulls slightly to the left," Micky told Sal.

Micky aimed again and hit the middle of the center mark. He aimed once more and had another perfect hit.

Micky grinned at Stacy. "Which stuffed animal do you want?" he asked.

"I want the unicorn," said Stacy pointing at the large pink unicorn.

The boy in the booth took a hook and retrieved the unicorn from the top row and handed it to Stacy with a smile. "Congratulations," he said with a smile.

"Thank you," said Stacy hugging her prize. She leaned in and kissed Micky. "Thank you for winning it for me," she whispered.

While they had been retrieving Stacy's prize, Sal had been checking out the gun. When the boy, in the booth, turned to Sal and Selma, Sal gave him money for three shots. Selma watched him. She was almost holding her breath. She was so excited. No one had ever tried to win a prize for her.

Sal, remembering Micky saying the gun pulled slightly to the left, aimed slightly to the right and fired three shots to the middle of the target. Selma clapped her hands in glee. Sal grinned at her. "Which animal do you want?" he asked.

Selma looked over the selections. "I want the giraffe," she said smiling.

The boy took down the giraffe and handed it to Selma. "Congratulations," he said. He looked at Sal and Micky. "You guys are really good at target shooting," he said.

"We have to be," responded Micky. "We are Avorn Security agents."

The boy smiled at the group. "Does Avorn have any job openings?" he asked.

"We are always looking for good agents. There is a lot of training involved. If you are interested go by the Avorn building and fill out an application," said Sal.

They told the boy goodbye and wandered on down the street. After buying some cotton candy, they stopped at a display. There was a big hammer. The person had to swing the hammer and hit the target. It would send the disc to the top and ring the bell. They were standing looking at it when Selma looked down and saw a little girl, about three years old, with tears running down her face. Selma kneelt to her level and gently put an arm around the little girl.

"What's wrong? Are you hurt?" asked Selma.

The girl shook her head. Sal kneelt beside Selma. "Are you lost?" he asked.

The girl shook her head again. "My momma is lost," she said. "I can't find her. Can you help me find my momma?" she asked.

Sal looked around and spotted a security guard watching them. He waved the guard over. The guard came over and looked at them suspiciously.

Sal took out his wallet and showed the guard his Avorn badge.

"This little ladies' momma is lost. Do you think you could help us find her?" he asked. The guard smiled. "I'm sure we can," he said smiling at the little girl and taking out his walkie talkie to call the other guards.

Sal squatted beside Selma, who was still comforting the little girl. "My name is Sal. Can you tell me your name?" he asked.

The little girl nodded. "My name is Delores," she said.

"I'm happy to meet you, Delores," said Sal. "Do you know your momma's name?"

Delores nodded. "Her name is Momma," she said. Selma and Stacy laughed. Sal, Micky, and the guard smiled.

Just then they heard a distraught voice call out, "Delores". They stood to see a young woman being led their way by another security guard. She broke away from the guard and ran to Delores. She grabbed her and hugged her tight. After a minute, she looked up at the group. "Thank you for finding Delores. I don't know how she disappeared so fast."

"You are welcome," said Sal. "Delores, whenever you are out with your momma, you have to keep a close watch on her. You would not want her to get lost again."

Delores smiled and nodded. "I will, Mr. Sal," she said. She leaned forward and gave him a hug. "Thank you for finding Momma for me," she said.

With another heartfelt thank you, Delores' mom took her hand and lead her away.

After they watched them leave, Selma turned and hugged Sal.

"Thank you for helping," said the guard. He grinned at Sal. "I'll have to remember your words when I caution my girls. I think they will be much more aware if they are told to make sure their mom doesn't get lost," he said.

Sal smiled. "I heard Alex Avorn tell a youngster that one time. It stuck in my mind," said Sal.

The guard went back to his duties and Sal turned to his group. "Are you ready for a ride on the ferris-wheel?" he asked.

Selma and Stacy looked over to where the attendant was unloading some passengers. Selma looked up where the wheel was taking people for a ride. "They are really high," she said uncertainly.

Sal squeezed her hand and held her close. "I'll be right beside you. You will be perfectly safe," he said.

"Okay," agreed Selma smiling at Sal.

Micky looked at Stacy. Stacy nodded with a grin. "I love the ferris-wheel. I haven't ridden one in years."

Sal and Micky led the way over to the ticket booth. They bought tickets and returned to get in line for a ride. There were only two couples ahead of them, so they did not have to wait long. Micky and Stacy were helped into their seat. The stuffed unicorn was seated beside her, making her squeeze closer to Micky. The attendant fastened the safety bar in front of them.

Selma waved at Stacy as the wheel moved forward. She and Sal were helped into the next seat. Sal made sure Selma's giraffe was safely fastened in beside her, when the attendant locked the bar in front of them. Selma held tightly to Sal's hand as the wheel started to move. Sal put his other arm around her and pulled her close to his side.

Micky and Stacy glanced back at them and Stacy gave Selma an encouraging smile. The wheel started to move, and Selma drew a deep breath. She looked up at Sal. Sal leaned over and kissed her. Selma forgot about the moving seat. When Sal was kissing her, all she thought about was Sal. When he raised his head, they were going over the top and starting down the other side.

"Oh my," whispered Selma hiding her face against Sal after one quick look down.

Sal chuckled and kissed her again. He felt her relax. When Sal ended the kiss, they had passed the bottom and were halfway up the other side. Selma didn't look down this time. She gazed at Sal. "Thank you," she whispered.

Thank me for what?" asked Sal.

Selma smiled. "Thank you for keeping me from having a panic attack," she said.

"It was my pleasure," assured Sal. "It is the best way to ride the ferris-wheel. I get to kiss you all I want to, and no one will say anything about it."

Selma laughed. "Is that why you wanted to go on this ride?" she asked.

Sal shook his head. "I wanted you to enjoy things you didn't have access to in Cendera," explained Sal.

Selma nodded. "The people of Cendera don't know what they are missing," she said.

The ferris wheel stopped, the attendant opened the bar, and Sal helped Selma out. They found Stacy and Micky waiting for them with big smiles on their faces.

"Well, how did you like it?" asked Stacy looking at Selma.

"It was great as long as Sal was kissing me," said Selma.

Stacy, Micky and Sal laughed.

"It is the only way to ride the Ferris-wheel," agreed Stacy

"Are you guys ready to go? I think I have had about enough of the fair," said Sal.

Stacy laughed. "There is never a dull moment with you guys," she said. Micky pulled her close to his side. "We try to please," he said.

Selma smiled at Sal. "Thank you for stopping at the fair," she said.

Sal and Micky held onto the girls and led them toward the parking lot.

When they were helping the girls into the car, Sal's phone rang. Sal looked at the screen before answering.

"Hello, Alex," said Sal. He stiffened and listened for a minute. "As soon as we drop the girls off at my folks house, Micky and I will go to help," said Sal.

Sal looked at Stacy. My folks house is not too far from here. "We have an emergency. Micky and I are needed. We will take you home when we come back," he said.

"Okay," Stacy agreed.

Sal started the car and drove quickly to his parents' house. He stopped at the curve and helped Selma out of the car. He quickly kissed her and promised to see her as soon as he could. Micky was helping Stacy out. When Micky climbed into the front seat beside Sal, Sal quickly drove away.

"What's is going on?" asked Micky.

"Andrew and Nelson were checking out a child trafficking house. They were shot at. Andrew was hit and Nelson is pinned down. Alex has sent everyone he can spare, and the police are also there." Sal was talking while he drove.

Sal cursed. Micky looked at him enquiringly.

"Call Alex," he said. "Put him on speaker."

"Hello," answered Alex.

"We are almost there," said Sal. "I was just thinking. This could be a diversion. Make sure you have plenty of guards in the building and put the building on lock down until we know what's going on," said Sal.

"You may be right," answered Alex. "I'll take care of it. Thanks."

They both hung up and Sal and Micky stopped their car and ran to join Nelson. The ambulance was taking Andrew Salto, one of Avorn's agents, away.

"How bad is Andrew?" Sal asked Nelson when they reached him.

"He will be fine. It was a flesh wound," answered Nelson. He was using his car for a shield.

"We were ambushed," said Nelson. "Alex received a tip about this place. We didn't even get a chance to get close before they started shooting at us."

"Is there any sign of children?" asked Micky.

"I haven't seen any. The police are handling the back and some of our agents are around the sides," said Nelson.

"Has anyone inside tried to talk or make demands?" asked Sal.

"No, they just shoot ever so often." said Nelson.

"Like they are stalling," said Sal thoughtfully.

Nelson looked at Sal, startled. "Yeah," he agreed. "They want to keep us occupied. I wonder what they are up to."

"Sal called Alex and advised him to put Avorn building on lock down," said Micky.

"Good idea," agreed Nelson looking around his car at the house. A series of shots had just been fired.

"We need to find a way to get them out of the house," said Sal. "They could keep us tied down here indefinitely," said Sal.

A police officer came up behind them. "We are having no luck getting close to the back. It's like they had everything prepared to hold us off," he said.

"They set this up so carefully. They have to have provided a way for their escape," said Sal thoughtfully.

"I don't see how," said the police officer. "We have them surrounded. If anyone comes out, we will get them."

"Do you know if this house has a basement?" asked Sal.

"It probably does," answered the officer. This is Oklahoma. Most houses have basements to use as storm shelters."

Sal looked at the officer. "Have your men check any small houses close to the road or a short distance from the house. Tell them to check for any tunnel that could lead to the basement. If they find one, we may be able to surprise the shooters."

The officer hurried away to spread the word.

Nelson grinned at Sal and Micky. "I'm glad you guys showed up. I would never have thought to look for a tunnel."

"They may not have a tunnel. We just have to check," said Sal.

Nelson received a call on his walkie talkie. "We have some movement at a side window," said one of their agents.

"Don't let then spot you," said Micky. "We don't want any more of you getting shot."

"He didn't see me. I am up a tree. I had a good view of the room when he looked out. I didn't see any children. I caught a glimpse of two other men," said the agent.

"Keep watching, but stay hidden," said Micky.

Nelson received a call from the police officer on his walkie talkie. "We found the tunnel entrance. It's in a small shed behind the house the shed is backed by a wooded area," said the officer.

"Are you going to wait for them to come out?" asked Nelson.

"We heard some movement. I am going to have my men hide and catch them as they come out," said the officer.

The guys drew back as there was more gunfire from the front of the house.

"They are trying to focus our attention on the front while they leave through the tunnel," said Micky.

Sal grinned. "They are in for a surprise," he said grimly.

It was only a short time later, when the police officers brought three men around to the front of the house. They were in handcuffs and heavily guarded.

The prisoners were placed in police cars to be transported. They looked sullen.

Sal's phone rang. "Hi, Alex. The shooters are in custody." Sal listened for a minute, then smiled widely. "Alex said they caught six men trying to enter Avorn security. They let them enter the elevator and then put them to sleep. They are being removed by the police. He arranged with the chief to have Trey there when they are questioned. Alex wants to know why they were attacking us."

The police officers, who were standing around listening, all laughed. "These men were trying to keep us busy so their friends could attack Avorn Security," he said.

Sal and Micky nodded.

"Why would they do anything so stupid?" asked another officer.

Everyone laughed. "There are a lot of bad people in the world," said Sal. He shook his head. "We can only do what we can to help save our city and its people"

The officers started coming by and shaking Avorn agent's hands and saying thank you, before leaving to transport the prisoners to jail.

Nelson smiled at Sal and Micky. Thanks for coming to help. I am headed to the hospital to check on Andrew."

"Tell him we will see him soon," said Micky.

Nelson entered his car and left.

Micky looked at Sal. "Can we go check on our girls?" he asked.

Sal smiled and started for the car. "We will be there in a few minutes," he said.

CHAPTER 10

Selma and Stacy watched Sal and Micky drive away before entering the house. Mrs. Mase was sitting on the sofa knitting. She looked up at them and smiled. She looked surprised when she looked behind them and saw no sign of Sal and Micky.

"Sal had an emergency call from Mr. Avorn. He said they would be here as soon as they take care of the emergency," Selma explained. "Mrs. Mase, this is Stacy Clark. She is Micky's true love. Their guardian angels said so."

Mrs. Mase laughed. "Hello, Stacy. Micky is a great young man. You will not be sorry your guardian angel matched you with him."

"It is nice to meet you," said Stacy. "Everything I have learned about Micky, tells me I am very lucky," agreed Stacy.

Mrs. Mase looked at the large pink unicorn Stacy was carrying. She saw Selma was holding a large giraffe. "Where in the world did those come from?" she asked laughing.

Stacy and Selma laughed and hugged their animals. "Sal and Micky won them for us in a shooting booth at a street fair," said Selma with a grin.

Mrs. Mase laughed. "It seems that their target practice has paid off," she remarked. "Would you girls like something to eat?"

"No, thank you. We ate at Holiday's," said Selma.

"Holiday's," said Mrs. Mase. "I have a large pitcher of ice-tea in the refrigerator."

Selma and Stacy laughed. "It seems you have been to Holiday's before," remarked Stacy.

Mrs. Mase nodded. "A few times," she agreed. "There is also some ice-cream in the freezer. It can help neutralize the spices."

"We are okay," said Selma. "Stacy and I are going to my room, so I can do my homework while we are waiting on Sal and Micky," said Selma.

Mrs. Mase nodded. "If you change your mind about the tea or ice-cream, help yourself," she remarked with a smile as she continued her knitting.

"We will, thank you," agreed Selma. She led the way to her room while Stacy followed.

When they entered the room, they laid their animals on Selma's bed. They stood back and smiled. The animals almost covered half the bed. Selma pulled out a chair for Stacy and opened her book bag to remove her homework.

Selma looked at her work. "I think I will do this later," she said. "Why don't we just talk while we wait?"

"I would like that," said Stacy. "I want to hear more about your hometown."

"Well," said Selma. "Cendera is hard to believe. It is a town where most of its residents have vigilante powers."

"What is vigilante power?" asked Stacy.

"It is the power to punish people for doing wrong or hurting someone," said Selma.

"How do they punish them?" asked Stacy.

Selma looked thoughtful for a moment, then smiled at Stacy before speaking.

"I overheard two women from Cendera talking about putting a

spell on a man. He was a bad flirt and he made his wife miserable. The spell would make him break out in hives whenever he flirted with any woman except his wife. It would not go away until he did something nice for his wife. The rash would come back if he flirted again," concluded Selma.

Stacy burst into laughter. "That could come in handy," she remarked.

Selma joined in the laughter. "Yes, it could," she agreed.

"Do you have vigilante power?" asked Stacy.

"Some," said Selma shaking her head. "Mostly I inherited my Great-Grandfather's mage power. I don't want anyone to know about me being a mage. If the witch hunters heard about it, they would be after me."

"I won't tell anyone," promised Stacy. "You haven't told me where Cendera is located."

"You would not be able to find it," said Selma. "Cendera is not listed on any map. There is no way in or out by regular means. It is invisible to outsiders. Once a person is inside Cendera, they can see everything in town and the surrounding countryside. The only way in or out is teleportation."

Stacy looked astonished. "You're kidding," she said.

"No, I am not," assured Selma. "You cannot tell anyone about Cendera. It might cause trouble for the town. No one would believe you anyway." Selma finished with a shrug.

"I won't tell a soul. My goodness. Do you suppose I might get a chance to visit there someday?" she asked.

"I don't know. Alex Avorn might be able to arrange something. I don't want to go back there anytime soon. The council might decide not to let me leave. They don't know about my powers and I don't know if my powers are strong enough to leave without their permission," said Selma.

Stacy sat back and stared at Selma wide-eyed. "I am going to love being neighbors with you and Sal. It is sure not going to be dull." She said with a laugh.

"I am glad we are going to be neighbors and friends, too. I have felt very alone most of my life," said Selma.

"You are not alone anymore. You have Sal, his family, Micky and me, and the Avorn family. You might be wishing for some alone time," said Stacy.

"I don't think so," disagreed Selma. "Although I might be wishing I didn't have to deal with my father before we settle matters between us"

Stacy nodded. "I know how hard it is to deal with family. My mother is a very major problem for me," she admitted.

"I know your mother is the district attorney," said Selma.

"Yes, her being the district attorney is not the problem. She is not a maternal person. She always makes sure she is in charge where-ever she is. Her word is law and she will not accept any opinion but hers. She has made life difficult for me and my brother all our lives. It is the main reason my brother joined the Navy instead of going to college. He wanted to be away from her," concluded Stacy.

Selma looked at Stacy sadly. "I did not grow up with my father. He dumped me on my aunt and left Cendera when my mother died. I was only six years old when he left. I didn't hear anything from him until a few days ago. He found out I was here, and he came looking for me."

"It is good he wanted to see you," commented Stacy.

Selma shook her head. "He was looking to take my mother's magic mirror from me. He had already stolen the one he sold your mother. He also took all of Mother's jewelry and what cash he could find when he left. He tried to get on my good side by telling me I had two brothers. He said he wanted me to meet them."

"You do want to meet your brothers, don't you? I don't know what I would have done if I had not been able to have my brother in my life," said Stacy.

"Yes," agreed Selma. "I am going to arrange a way to get to know my brothers, but I am not going to give my father a free pass to rob me."

Stacy looked at Selma with a sad expression. "Why does life have to be so complicated?" she asked.

Selma smiled and shook her head. "I didn't mean to make you sad. After all, we have a lot to be happy about. We have two great guys. We are going to the prom and we are about to start a wonderful life in our new homes with our guys," stated Selma.

"Yes, we are," agreed Stacy perking up.

"Would you like some ice cream or tea?" asked Selma. "We could take it into the front room and visit with Mrs. Mase."

"Okay," agreed Stacy. "I wonder how long Micky and Sal will be?"

Selma lad the way to the kitchen.

"I don't know, but I hope they are alright," said Selma as she removed the ice cream from the freezer. Selma took three bowls from the cabinet and spoons from the drawer. After putting a generous helping in each bowl and returning the ice cream to the freezer, Selma handed one bowl to Stacy. She carried the other two bowls and led the way to the living room.

"We decided the ice cream sounded like a good idea," Selma informed Mrs. Mase. "I brought you a bowl." Selma handed one bowl to Mrs. Mase.

Mrs. Mase put aside her knitting and accepted the bowl with a smile. "Thank you." Mrs. Mase savored a bite and smiled as she watched Selma and Stacy enjoying their bowls of ice cream.

She watched Selma sit still for a moment staring into space before smiling to herself.

Selma looked up and saw Mrs. Mase watching her. Selma smiled. "Sal and Micky are on their way. They are okay," said Selma.

"How do you know?" asked Stacy.

"Sal told me," said Selma.

Stacy looked puzzled. "How? I didn't hear the phone ring."

"Sal and I can pass messages to each other in our minds. We don't have to call on the phone," said Selma.

"Wow!" exclaimed Stacy. "Do you think Micky and I will be able to talk to each other in our minds?" asked Stacy.

"It's possible," said Selma. "I think it has something to do with our guardian angels."

Selma shrugged. "Maybe they pass along our thoughts for us."

"It would be so cool," said Stacy dreamily.

Mrs. Mase nodded and smiled as she listened to the girls talk. "It is very cool," she agreed.

When the ice cream was eaten, Mrs. Mase started to rise to take the bowls. Selma hurriedly rose and took the bowls. "I'll take these and put them in the dishwasher," she said.

"Alright," agreed Mrs. Mase sitting back and taking up her knitting again.

Selma carried the three bowls into the kitchen. After giving them a rinse, Selma placed the bowls in the dishwasher. She could hear Stacy and Mrs. Mase talking quietly in the living room. When Selma turned to go into the living room, the door to the garage opened and Sal and Micky entered.

Sal quickly put his arms around Selma and kissed her. Micky passed them and went to the living room to find Stacy.

After Selma returned his kiss, she leaned back in his arms and investigated his face. "Are you alright?" she asked.

"I'm fine," said Sal kissing her again.

When he let her come up for air, Selma put up a hand to stop him from kissing her again. "We need to join the others in the living room. Your mom will be wondering what is taking so long," said Selma.

Sal grinned. "I'm sure she can guess what is taking so long," he said as he let Selma lead him into the living room.

Mrs. Mase looked at Sal searchingly as he entered the room. "Are you alright?" she asked. "Micky said you were both involved in a gun fight."

"A gunfight!" exclaimed Selma, looking at Sal.

"We are fine. It wasn't a gunfight. The men ambushed Nelson

and Andrew. They were trying to draw the guards away from Avorn so they could get inside the building. We stayed behind cover while they shot their guns to keep us occupied," said Sal. He gave Selma's hand a reassuring squeeze.

"Are Nelson and Andrew alright?" asked Mrs. Mase.

"Nelson is fine. Andrew had a flesh wound. He was treated at the hospital and released," said Sal.

"Why were they trying to get into Avorn?" asked Selma holding tightly to Sal's hand.

"We don't know. They were all arrested. Alex sent Trey to the police station to be there while they are questioned. He wants to know what they were after," said Micky.

"Alex will let us know when he finds out what they were after," stated Sal. "Everything will be fine." Sal gently rubbed Selma's neck under her hair. Selma looked into his eyes. She loved the feel of Sal's hand on her, but she felt a little self- conscious with everyone watching.

Sal led her to a chair and sitting down, drew Selma down into his lap. Selma sat stiffly at first, then, when she saw no one was paying any attention, she relaxed against him and felt his arms close around her.

Sal smiled at Micky who was sitting in a chair close enough to Stacy to hold her hand. Micky looked at Selma sitting in Sal's lap and wished he had Stacy in his lap.

"Where's Dad?" asked Sal.

"He is meeting with the men's group at church. They are working on doing a fundraiser for a family down on their luck," said Mrs. Mase.

"I'm surprised the ladies' group isn't in charge," said Sal with a smile.

"We decided to let the men handle this one. I think they were feeling a little left out of things with the women always being in charge," said Mrs. Mase smiling.

Sal laughed and shook his head. "What are you ladies up to? You know the ladies have the fundraising well in hand."

Mrs. Mase just smiled. "Don't you worry about it. We have everything under control," she remarked.

"It's fine," said Sal. "My lips are sealed. I won't say another word."

Mrs. Mase smiled. She was used to her boys teasing her. She did not let it bother her.

Sal's phone rang. When he looked at it and saw Alex was calling, he answered. "Hi, Alex," said Sal. He listened for a few minutes without speaking. "Okay Alex. Micky and I will meet Trey there."

Sal hung up the phone and helped Selma up so he could stand. Micky was already standing. Sal looked at Stacy. "Could you stay here with Selma tonight? You can ride the bus to school in the morning. Micky and I will pick both of you after school tomorrow."

"Sure, if it is okay with Selma and your mom," replied Stacy.

"You are welcome to stay." said Mrs. Mase. She looked at Sal. "What is going on?" asked Mrs. Mase.

Alex found out the men trying to get in the building were sent by the child traffickers. They were unhappy with Alex being able to free so many of their captives. Alex found out where there is a group of children being held. He is organizing a raid to free them. We have to go," said Sal kissing Selma quickly and heading for the door.

"Be careful," said Selma. "Bring those children home."

"We will," promised Sal. He and Micky hurried out the door.

Selma glanced at Stacy. She saw how worried Stacy looked and going over to her, Put an arm around her shoulder. "They will be alright," said Selma.

"Is it always like this?" asked Stacy.

Mrs. Mase came over to the girls and put an arm around each. I think the waiting will go much faster if we have a small snack," she said encouraging the girls toward the kitchen.

"I don't know if I can eat anything," admitted Selma. "My stomach is tied in knots."

"I never saw the knots that could not be untied with a piece of chocolate cake," said Mrs. Mase going to the cabinet and retrieving three plates. Selma placed three forks on the plates while Mrs. Mase cut three pieces of cake. They all looked up when the garage door opened, and Mr. Mase came in.

"Don't forget to cut me a slice," he said looking at the slices of cake.

Mrs. Mase obediently cut another slice while Selma fetched another plate and fork.

They all sat at the table and ate their cake while They filled Mr. Mase in on Sal and Micky.

Mr. Mase gazed around the table at the worried faces. "Alex makes sure all the agents working for Avorn are very well trained. He will not let anyone work for him until he is sure they are as safe as he can make them. Sal and Micky have been working for Avorn for many years. They will be careful. They had to go. Knowing about the children, they had to try and free them. It's the type of men they are. "

All three ladies were nodding. "We know," agreed Selma. "We wouldn't love them so much if they were different."

They finished their cake and rinsing the plates, placed them in the dishwasher.

"When I told Sal, I would stay the night, I didn't think about what I would wear to school tomorrow," said Stacy.

Selma looked at Stacy. We are about the same size. We can see if I have anything you can wear. I will also find you something to sleep in."

"Are you a student at Selma's school?" asked Mr. Mase.

Stacy shook her head, "No, Sir, I am a student teacher," remarked Stacy.

"Oh," said Mr. Mase looking puzzled.

"Stacy is Micky's girl. Their guardian angels matched them," explained Mrs. Mase.

"Oh," Mr. Mase smiled. "Welcome to our family, Stacy. Micky has been an honorary member for years, Now, you are also."

"Thank you," said Stacy flushing with pleasure. "I am very happy to be an honorary member of your family."

The girls took their leave, so Selma could find Stacy something to wear and finish her homework.

CHAPTER 11

Sal and Micky pulled in behind another agent's car and quietly exited their car. They joined the other agent, who was waiting for others to arrive, He was watching the house to make sure the children were not moved before they could be freed.

"Is anything happening?" asked Micky.

"No," answered the agent. "There has been no movement since I arrived. Alex said one of the leaders was watching this group. If at all, possible, he wants him caught."

"I know," agreed Sal. "Alex really wants to get his hands on him. He gets angry when anyone preys on small children. It takes a certain type of callousness to target the young. The cowards can't pick on anyone who can fight back."

Micky and the agent silently agreed with Sal. They were unable to comprehend the child trafficking business. It was an abomination on society. It seemed some people were born with something missing inside them.

They looked around as Trey joined them. Sal and Micky greeted Trey quietly.

"Do you know who is in the house?" asked Micky.

"I was told the man in charge of this area is here. He is planning for the children to be picked up before morning. He likes to move them at night, so they draw less attention. We want to stop him before they are moved," said Trey. "Brenda pulled up the plans for this house. The men said the children were being kept in the basement. According to the plans, there is a coal chute behind the house. It hasn't been used in a long time, but it may be our way into the basement. It would be good if we could remove the children before arresting the men in charge."

"Are we expecting any help?" asked Sal.

"The SWAT team is getting into position," said Trey. "They know we are going to try and get the children out first. Alex has called in more Avorn agents, also. I imagine they will be joining us shortly."

Sal looked at Trey. "Micky and I will make our way around back and see if we can enter the basement. You wait here, and when our agents arrive, send them to help with the children."

"Okay, you need to call me when you are in position, before you go inside," agreed Trey. "Alex wants me to talk to the man in charge if I get a chance."

"We will worry about him after we rescue the children," said Sal.

Trey nodded and Micky and Sal slipped away to make their way to the back of the house without being seen. On the way around the house, Sal and Micky were joined by three members of the SWAT Team. They had worked with the men before.

"Hi, Lance," Sal greeted one of the men. He was most familiar with Lance, although he had met the other two, Fred and John. Sal and Micky nodded a greeting to Fred and John. Lance reached into his vest and drew out two Swat vests.

"I brought you and Micky a vest each, to wear, so you won't be accidentally shot by any of our team," said Lance handing them the vests. Sal and Micky grinned as they put on the vests.

"Thanks, Lance," said Micky.

"Why are we headed behind the house?" asked one of the team.

They were following Sal and Micky to the back of the house.

"The plans for the house show a coal chute back here. It leads into the basement, where we think the children are being held. We may be able to get them out before the shooting starts," said Sal. "Here it is." Sal was kneeling beside the chute. It was wooden with a large lock on it.

"If we try to break the lock, the men up front will hear us," said Lance.

Sal smiled as he pulled a large skeleton key from his pocket. "I thought this might come in handy," he said as he fit it into the lock and, after jiggling it a bit, the lock popped open.

He lay the lock on the ground and put the key back in his pocket. Sal and Fred quietly lifted the wooden door.

"Who's there?" asked a young male voice from inside. He was keeping his voice low.

Fred held the door up and found a piece of wood to prop it open. Sal knelt and stuck his head inside. "We are working with the police. We are going to get you out of here," said Sal. "How many children are here?"

"There are twelve, counting myself and my sister. My name is Jerry. My sister is Joyce," He answered.

"My name is Sal. Do you think you could hand the children up to me one at a time?"

"Sure," said Jerry. He was standing on a wooden box under the opening. Jerry turned and asked his sister to hand him one of the young children. She handed one to him, and he held the child up to Sal. Sal pulled the child out and handed her to one of the seal team.

"When I hand you another child, take them to safety and send someone else back to help. We have twelve children to rescue." Sal turned to receive the next child. Jerry was ready, holding the next child up to Sal. Sal passed the child to Micky and Micky passed him over to be taken to safety.

Jerry passed the children up, and Sal passed them on. They worked quickly. Finally, the small children had been passed out and

Jerry picked up his sister and held her up to be rescued. After passing Joyce to Micky, Sal looked at Jerry. "If you hold up your arms, I will pull you out," said Sal.

Jerry reached up with his arms, but he wasn't tall enough to reach Sal's hands.

Sal tried reaching, but he could not reach Jerry. Sal looked at Micky. "Do you and Lance think you can hold my legs and pull me and Jerry out. The only way I am going to be able to reach him is by leaning down inside,"

Lance and Micky, each, grabbed one of Sal's legs, Sal scooted forward into the opening and leaning down grabbed Jerry's hands. "Okay pull," said Sal. Micky and Lance started pulling on Sal's legs. They eased him back and Sal held onto Jerry's hands and eased him out of the opening.

When they were safely out, Sal and Jerry lay, breathing hard. Sal reached and gave Jerry a hug. Then, Sal lowered the door and put the lock back on it. He smoothed the ground around the door, so the escape route would not be discovered. Jerry stood back and watched Sal and Micky work.

"Thanks for helping us rescue the children," said Sal.

"Thanks for getting us out of there," said Jerry. "I didn't think we had any chance of getting out alive." Jerry looked around. "Where is my sister?" he asked.

"She is with the children at the SWAT van. They will all be taken to the hospital to be checked before their parents are called to come and get them," said Sal.

Jerry shook his head as Sal and Micky led him away from the house. They were on their way to the van.

"How old are you, Jerry?" asked Micky.

"I'm twelve and my sister is nine. We do not have any parents. We were in foster care. Two of the other kids were in the foster home we were in," said Jerry. I think the sleaze sold them to the traffickers. I slipped Joyce out of there when the sleaze tried to molest her. We were living on the street when we were captured."

"Who is the Sleaze?" asked Sal.

"He is Mrs. Marks' husband. She the head of the foster home. She is okay, but he is horrible. Me and Joyce are not going back there," said Jerry determinedly.

Sal put an arm around Jerry's shoulder as they arrived at the van.

Lance had been walking with them and had heard Jerry's comments. He looked at Sal. "What do you want to do?" Lance asked Sal.

"I want to take Joyce and Jerry with me and Micky. We will let Alex handle everything," Sal concluded grimly. "There is no way I am taking these children back to those people."

Lance chuckled softly. He looked in the van and asked Joyce to come out and join her brother. Joyce happily scrambled out and hurried over and hugged Jerry.

"Are you sure you should let them take them?" asked the SWAT officer who was watching the children in the van.

Lance looked at him sternly. "They were never here," said Lance as he watched Sal and Micky disappear with Joyce and Jerry. "Alex Avorn will take care of everything. Those kids don't know it, but this was their lucky day. They will be brought to the attention of Alex Avorn." Lance smiled and closed the door of the van. "Take these children to the hospital. We have some bad guys to catch," said Lance.

Trey smiled when Sal and Micky arrived wearing SWAT vests, with two children in tow.

"Have you two joined the SWAT team?" asked Trey.

"Lance gave us the vests to keep us from being accidentally shot," said Micky.

"I thought you guys were SWAT," said Jerry. "If you are not SWAT, who are you?"

"We help the SWAT team, but we are agents for Avorn Security," said Sal. "Our boss, Alex Avorn will help you and your sister to avoid being sent back to the sleaze." Sal looked Jerry in the eyes. "I promise we will take care of you both. You are safe with us."

Jerry stared back at him, then he smiled. " I believe you," he said.

"Good," said Sal. "Trey I am going to take them to my mom. I'll be back as soon as I can. Micky, you want to stay here and help?"

"Okay," agreed Micky. "Tell Stacy I'm alright, and I'll see her tomorrow."

"Okay," agreed Sal. He opened the door of his car and helped Joyce and Jerry into the back seat. He watched them fasten their seat belts before getting in the front and heading for his parents' home.

When Sal arrived at his parent's house, he drove into the garage before getting the children out. When he entered the kitchen with Jerry and Joyce, his parents looked up from where they were sitting at the table. Mr. and Mrs. Mase rose and went to Sal and the children.

"Mom is it alright for Jerry and Joyce to stay here tonight? I need to get back and help Micky and the team. I didn't want them taken to the hospital until I can talk to Alex. They are in a bad situation in their foster home. I didn't want to take a chance on them being sent back there," said Sal. He had an arm around each child and was looking at his parents expectantly.

"Salvadori Mase, of course it's alright. Where else would you take them?" she asked coming over and putting an arm around each child. Mr. Mase chuckled. "You know you can depend on us to help, Sal," he agreed.

Selma and Stacy entered the kitchen. They had heard Sal's voice. Stacy looked around. "Where's Micky?" she asked.

"He's with our agents. They are watching the house where the children were being held," said Sal. He came over and gave Selma a hug. "I have to get back and help. Micky wanted me to tell you he is alright, and he will see you tomorrow," Sal told Stacy. "I have to go," he whispered to Selma giving her a quick kiss before turning to Jerry. "I'll see you tomorrow. You and Joyce are safe here and I promise you will not have to return to the Sleaze."

Jerry looked up at Sal with hero worship in his eyes. "Thanks for saving us," he said.

Sal smiled and hugged him before leaving out the garage door.

"Be careful," Selma thought in her head as Sal left.

"I will," promised Sal in her thoughts.

Sal quickly returned to the stakeout. He found Micky and Nelson standing with the other Avorn agents. The Avorn agent was talking to a SWAT team member on the phone.

"There looks like we have some visitors," said the agent as a van pulled to a stop in front of the house. Three men exited the van and entered the front door. The person inside, did not expose himself when he opened the door. He stood behind the door, so it was not possible to get a clear shot at him.

The men were inside only about five minutes when the teams outside, heard gunshots from inside. The men from the van came rushing through the door into the arms of the team. They were quickly disarmed and handcuffed. The men were sitting on the ground with guns pointing at them, when Sal, Micky, and the other Avorn agents joined them. Trey was with the SWAT team.

The Swat team led the way inside. They found two men lying on the floor. They had been shot. One was dead and the other was badly hurt. "I guess the new guys did not like finding the merchandise missing," said one of the SWAT team members in amusement.

"I guess not," agreed Trey. "I don't think I will be getting any useful information from these two. Maybe I can find out something useful from the men outside." Trey turned and went outside.

Everyone was in a hurry to get away from the men inside. They considered the men had gotten what they deserved for preying on children. They did call an ambulance for the one still alive, but they told the ambulance not to hurry.

Outside, Trey walked over to where the men were sitting on the ground. He concentrated on the youngest member of the group. "You want to tell me what happened in the house," said Trey. Trey was concentrating on contacting the man's guardian angel. While he was asking the man a few simple questions to keep him occupied, Trey was finding out all he needed from the man's guardian angel.

When Trey looked up, he turned to the SWAT team. "The man

in the red sweater is in charge. He ordered the men inside shot, when they could not produce the children they had promised. He thought they were being set up," concluded Trey.

The men on the ground looked at Trey in astonishment. "How do you know?" the man in the red sweater demanded. "He did not tell you anything. What are you, a mind reader?"

Trey laughed. "No, I am not a mind reader. Your guardian angels told me. They do not like what you are doing. I agree with your guardian angels. I don't like what you are doing either. So, from now on, you are going to find a new profession. First, you are going to confess to the police and take the punishment you deserve."

The men on the ground looked at Trey blankly before lowering their heads and not saying anything else. The SWAT team loaded the men into police cars to be transported to police headquarters.

Lance turned to Sal, Micky and Trey. "Thanks for your help. I really appreciate the help getting the children to safety," he said.

"It was our pleasure. We'll see you next time," said Sal with a laugh. They removed the vests and returned them to lance with a thank you. They shook hands and Lance before he left.

Sal and Micky turned to Trey. The other Avorn agents were joining them. "Is it over, or do you need us for more?" asked Nelson of Trey.

Trey looked around at the group. "You can all go home but check in with Alex tomorrow. He will want a report from each of you," said Trey.

The agents started leaving. They were thankful it was over with only the bad guys being hurt. There were some police at the house handling the shooting. They were not needed.

Trey started to his car. He stopped and looked at Sal. "Did you leave those two kids with your mom?" he asked.

Sal nodded. "I have to talk to Alex tomorrow and see if he can help with them," said Sal.

"I'm sure he will. Alex always has the answer," said Trey with a smile as he entered his car and drove away.

Sal and Micky entered their car and sat there for a minute thinking. "Do you think it is too late to go by and let everyone know it's over and we are alright?' asked Micky.

Sal smiled he had been mind talking with Selma.

"Selma says they are still up. The kids have had a bath, and Mom is feeding them. I told her we would be there in a few minutes," concluded Sal starting the car and heading for his parent's house.

When Sal and Micky entered the garage door a few minutes later, Selma and Stacy were waiting for them. The girls went straight into their arms and hugged their guys tight. They were making sure there were no injuries.

Mr. and Mrs. Mase, seated at the table with Jerry and Joyce, smiled in relief.

Jerry and Joyce looked on in amazement. It was hard for them to believe a family like this one existed.

Sal looked up and grinned at Jerry. "How are you and Joyce?" he asked.

"We are great," said Jerry.

We need to go and let you all get some sleep," said Sal looking at Selma. "We wanted you to know we were alright."

"I'm glad you stopped by. I'm glad you are alright," said Selma hugging him again.

"Me, too," agreed Stacy hugging Micky close. He didn't seem to have any objections.

Mrs. Mase nodded at Sal and Micky. "You two need to go and get some rest. I'm sending everyone to bed as soon as Jerry and Joyce finish eating," she said.

"Okay, Mom. Thanks for helping. I'll let you know what's going on after I talk to Alex in the morning," said Sal.

"I was glad to help," said Mrs. Mase looking fondly at Jerry and Joyce.

Sal and Micky gave their girls one quick last kiss and left through the garage door.

CHAPTER 12

Sal and Micky were at Avorn Security Building early the next morning. Sal had called his mom and told her not to send Jerry and Joyce to school until he had a chance to talk to Alex. He didn't want the school calling the foster home about them.

Lynn sent them into Alex's office when they arrived on the third floor. Trey was already in Alex's office talking with him. Alex smiled at them and motioned for them to take a seat.

"You two had a busy night," observed Alex. "I'm glad you were able to move the children safely."

"We need to talk to you about the children," said Sal.

Alex nodded. Trey told me you took two of them to your mom," said Alex.

Sal nodded. "They had run away from their foster home to keep the sister from being raped. She is only nine years old," added Sal in disgust. "Two more of the children rescued were from the same foster home. Jerry, the boy I carried to Mom, said Mr. Marks, the foster mom's husband, had sold those two girls to the traffickers."

Alex shook his head. "We can't send those children back until Marks is taken care of," he said.

Alex punched a button on his phone and received an immediate response from Lynn.

"Lynn would you connect me with Suzy Hamilton at Child Protective Services."

Alex turned to Sal while he was waiting to be connected. "Are you interested in something more permanent with Jerry and his sister?" he asked Sal.

Sal looked at him blankly. He had not thought about anything permanent. He just wanted the two to be safe. Jerry had touched something in him and was tugging at his heartstrings.

Before Sal could answer, the phone rang.

"Hello, Suzy, this is Alex Avorn." He put the phone on speaker, so everyone could hear the conversation.

"Hello, Alex, you are calling early. I suppose this has something to do with the group of children your agents helped rescue last night," answered Suzy.

"Yes, it does. There were two small children from the Marks foster home. It has come to my attention that Mr. Marks may have sold them to the traffickers," said Alex.

"Are you sure of your information?" asked Suzy.

"The information was given by a young boy. He ran away from the home with his nine- year- old sister to keep her from being raped by Mr. Marks," replied Alex.

"Would it be possible for me to talk to the boy and his sister?" asked Suzy.

"Not at this time. We are in the process of arranging a permanent home for the two and we don't want them back in the system. It is too hard to get them out once they are in," replied Alex.

Suzy paused for a minute. "You do know, there is no one else I would let get away with this," said Suzy with a chuckle.

"I appreciate that, Suzy," responded Alex grinning at Sal.

"Do you have any ideas about stopping Mr. Marks, without evidence?" asked Suzy.

"I have an idea," said Alex. "Why don't you pay a surprise visit to the Marks foster home. Make sure Mr. Marks is going to be there. Trey can go along with you as an assistant. Trey can see about changing Mr. Marks' way of thinking, and the way he is treating the children in the foster home. Trey can convince him to accept the proper punishment for his past acts against the children."

"I have worked with Trey before," responded Suzy. "I think it is an excellent idea." The men smiled. They could hear the satisfaction in Suzy's voice

"Let me know when you want to pay the visit. I will make sure Trey can accompany you," said Alex. "Try to make the visit before the two children at the hospital are returned to the home."

"I have them here. The hospital called me last night to pick them up. I haven't returned them to the foster home. I may be looking for new homes for them and the other children in the Marks home. I don't see how Mrs. Marks could have been unaware of what her husband was up to. That is unacceptable behavior for a foster home," concluded Suzy.

"Don't do anything until you are sure. According to my source, Mrs. Marks was okay. They only had a problem with the husband. I may be wrong, but with the need for foster care, it will pay you to be sure," said Alex.

Suzy sighed. "You may be right, I won't close the home until I'm sure, but I will be keeping a close watch on her and the worker assigned to investigate the Marks' home," concluded Suzy with force in her voice.

They hung up the phones and Alex looked at Trey. "I wouldn't want to be the worker in charge of the Marks foster home. Suzy is going to make her pay for missing so many signals in the home," said Alex. He looked over at Sal. "Well, have you thought about how you want to help Jerry and his sister?" asked Alex.

"I'll have to talk to Selma. It is an awful lot to ask of her. She is only eighteen and Jerry is twelve. We are not married, yet. I don't know how she would feel about starting out with a ready- made family," said Sal thinking out loud.

Alex smiled. "We have a little time. Talk to Selma. If she is against taking on a ready-made family, we have time to work on another solution," Alex concluded.

Sal thoughtfully nodded. "I'll talk to Selma after school today," he said.

Micky had been sitting quietly listening. He knew Sal wanted to help Jerry and his sister, but he did not envy him having to face a discussion with Selma about keeping the two permanently. Micky was glad he did not have to put such a proposal to Stacy.

"What's going to happen to the men arrested last night?" asked Micky.

Alex grinned. They confessed everything and are taking a plea bargain. District Attorney Mavis Clark is rubbing her hands in satisfaction and taking credit for everything. She gave a news conference earlier. You would think she personally went out and brought the bad guys in."

"She must be up for reelection," said Trey with a grin.

"Yes," agreed Alex. "She is."

Alex turned to Micky and Sal. "You two stay away from her, I don't want you on her radar. We don't want to deal with her. Let her take all the credit. It will keep the attention from being focused on us. We don't need anyone else trying to attack Avorn Building," Alex finished firmly.

"Have you told our guards to be on full alert?" asked Sal.

Alex nodded. "They are watching closely. Especially the ones watching the elevators. They have a fresh supply of sleeping gas installed," said Alex.

Sal, Micky, and Trey smiled and rose from their chairs.

"I'll let you know when I hear from Suzy," Alex said to Trey. Trey nodded and went out the door.

"Do you have anything for us to take care of today?" asked Micky.

"Yes, I want you to check at the hospital and be sure all of the children have been returned to their parents. If it's possible, I would like information on how the traffickers managed to get their hands on the children. I want to be sure we are not sending any of the children back into danger," concluded Alex.

"We are on it," agreed Sal. He and Micky left to make their way to the hospital.

Sal and Micky met Lance and a female SWAT team member coming out of the hospital as they started to enter.

"Hi, Lance, Hi, Slim," said Sal. Slim's name was Lou, but everyone called her Slim. "Has something else happened?" asked Sal.

"No," answered Lance. We were checking on the children. Slim and a female police officer stayed with them and gathered names and addresses from the parents when they picked up their children," said Lance.

"Have they all been picked up?" asked Micky.

"Six of them went home with their parents. Child Protective Services has taken the other four," answered Slim.

"How did the reunions go?" asked Sal.

"Most of them went great. You could see the parents were overjoyed to have their children returned," said Slim.

"Most, not all," remarked Sal.

Slim shrugged. "There was one little boy. He clung to the police officer and did not want to go with his mother," said Slim.

"Do you have the boy's name and address?" asked Sal.

"Yes," nodded Slim. She took out a piece of paper and wrote the boy's name and address down. She gave it to Sal.

"Thanks, Slim. I'll give this to Alex. He will want to check it out. He has already talked to Child Protective Services. He will be able to check on the children with them. Do you think you could get me a list of the other children? Alex will want to do a follow up with them to make sure they are alright," asked Sal.

"Sure, I'll get you a list and drop it off at the front desk of Avorn," said Slim.

"Thanks," said Sal with a smile.

"How are the two you took home with you?" asked Lance.

"They are fine. Alex is working on their situation now," answered Sal.

Lance nodded and grinned. "Did you tell Alex about the Sleaze?" asked Lance.

Micky and Sal laughed. "I don't think the word 'sleaze' was brought into the conversation, but Alex is aware of the situation," agreed Sal with a grin.

Lance looked at his watch. "We have to report in. If you need anything else, let us know. We will help any way we can," said Lance.

"Thanks. If you hear of any more situations like the one last night, or if you need our help, call us," said Sal. They all nodded goodbye and Lance and Slim departed.

"We don't need to go inside. We have the information we were looking for," said Micky.

"I think we need to go by and have lunch with Mom. I can talk to Jerry and Joyce and find out more about their situation. I don't even know their last names," said Sal.

"I'm always up for some of your mom's cooking," agreed Micky with a grin. They returned to their car and headed to the Mase home. Sal was trying to figure out what he wanted to do.

"How do I get myself into such situations?" he mused.

"It's because you care," responded Micky. "There are too many people in this world who don't care. The ones who do care are left trying to take up the slack for the others. It makes it very hard for some of us."

Sal glanced at Micky, before turning his attention back to the road. "I am glad I am in the group who cares," said Sal. "I wouldn't want to be without feeling for the children."

"I know, me either," Micky agreed.

Sal pulled the car into the garage, and he and Micky went inside. Mrs. Mase was in the kitchen when they entered. She turned, smiled at them, and accepted a hug from each. Then, she turned back to stirring the pan on the stove.

"Where are the kids?" asked Sal.

"They are in the living room watching television. There is a teaching program on PBS. Since they are missing school, I thought it was a good program for them to watch." Mrs. Mase turned and looked at Sal. "If they are going to be here for a while, we need to get them some clothes. They cannot keep wearing the same outfit. I washed their clothes while they were sleeping last night. The clothes will fall apart if they are washed every night," Mrs. Mase laughed.

"I'll get Selma to help me buy them some clothes," said Sal. Mrs. Mase looked at him sharply but did not comment.

"There is coffee made if you would like a cup," said Mrs. Mase to Micky and Sal.

Micky went over to the cabinet to fetch a cup while Sal sat at the counter. "Do you want a cup?" Micky asked Sal.

"No, thanks," Sal answered.

Mrs. Mase examined Sal. "Is something wrong?" she asked.

"I have a dilemma," said Sal. Mrs. Mase did not say anything. She waited patiently for Sal to continue. "Alex asked me if I wanted to do anything permanent with Jerry and Joyce," said Sal.

"What did you tell him?" asked Mrs. Mase.

"I told him I would have to talk to Selma," said Sal.

Mrs. Mase nodded. "Of course, you do," she agreed. "Are you hoping for anything permanent?"

Sal looked at her. "I would like to take those two kids and raise them. They are great kids. They stayed in the basement and helped hand up the others until they were all out before attempting to come out. You know they were scared and wanted out of there, but they helped rescue the others first. I just don't know if it is fair to expect Selma to take on a ready-made family when she is so young."

"You are not exactly ancient. You are only twenty-six," said Mrs. Mase with a smile.

"Yeah, but Selma is only eighteen," said Sal'

"I think you are borrowing trouble," said Micky. "You need to stop worrying until you can talk to Selma. She may be for the idea," protested Micky.

Jerry, standing just outside the dining room door, had heard the entire conversation. He hugged Sal's words to him and smiled. Sal wanted him and Joyce. No one had wanted them since their parents had died. Sal really wanted them. Jerry's eyes turned misty as he went back into the living room and sat down.

"You didn't get us a drink," said Joyce.

"No, Mrs. Mase was busy. She was talking to Sal and Micky. I did not want to interrupt," said Jerry. Joyce rose from her seat. "Where are you going?" asked Jerry.

"I'm thirsty. I'm going to ask for a drink," said Joyce. Jerry watched her go. He wasn't thirsty anymore. He was too happy inside.

"Hi, Joyce," said Sal when he spotted Joyce peeping around the door.

"Hi," said Joyce. Could I get a drink?" she asked.

"Sure," said Sal, going to the refrigerator and looking inside. "What would you like? We have chocolate milk, apple juice, or orange juice," he said.

"I like apple juice," said Joyce with a grin.

Sal took out an apple juice box. It had a straw in it. Sal fixed the straw in the box and handed it to Joyce.

"Thanks," said Joyce. She drew in a swallow and smiled at Sal.

"Why don't you sit here with Micky and enjoy your apple juice. I'll take Jerry a drink. Do you know which juice he likes?" asked Sal.

"He likes apple, too," said Joyce. She climbed onto the stool next to Micky and gave him a big smile. Micky smiled back and started asking her about the show she had been watching on television.

Sal took another apple juice box and went into the living room to talk to Jerry. He decided it was a good time to learn more about these two, before he talked to Selma.

"Hi, I thought you could use a drink," said Sal.

"Thanks," said Jerry taking the juice with a smile.

"You know, I completely forgot to ask you your last name. It was so confusing, I guess we never thought of asking," said Sal.

"I didn't want to say my last name in front of the police," said

Jerry with a grin. "It's Lawson. My parents were missionaries. Sandra and Louis Lawson. They were caught in an uprising in the village where they were preaching, and they were killed. They had left me and Joyce with my dad's sister, Thelma. When she heard they were killed, she turned us over to Child Protective Service. She said, since Dad was no longer able to send her a monthly check, she was not going to take responsibility for anyone else's mistakes," Jerry looked at Sal as if it didn't matter what his aunt had done or said, but Sal could tell that he had been hurt deeply by his aunt's attitude.

Sal reached over and pulled Jerry into a hug. He didn't say anything. He just sat there quietly letting Jerry know he was not alone. Joyce, coming into the room, looked surprised to see Sal hugging Jerry. She smiled at Sal. Sal smiled back and raised an arm to her. Joyce hurried over and Sal pulled her into the hug. Sal didn't know how he was going to do it, but he had to convince Selma these two kids needed them and their love.

Micky and Mrs. Mase started into the room but stopped when they saw Sal and the children in a group hug. They stood there smiling at the sight of this large, strong guy being so emotional with the children.

CHAPTER 13

*S*elma was distracted in her classes. She had been thinking about the children all day. She was worried about what was going to happen to them. She hated the idea of them being sent back into foster care. They needed a home and someone to love them and let them know they were important. They were good kids. Selma sighed. She didn't know if she and Sal could help them. They were not married, yet. They probably would not be allowed to take the children. Selma shook her head. She did not know how Sal would feel about helping the children. She would have to talk to him. This day was passing so slow. It seemed as if the time would never pass.

"Patience," said her guardian angel. "You do not have to worry. Everything is as it should be. Love is the answer to any dilemma."

"What does that mean?" wondered Selma. Sometimes it was hard to understand her guardian angel. Selma sighed and tried to pay attention to her teacher. She would have to wait until school was out to talk to Sal.

"Lunch is ready," said Mrs. Mase.

Jerry and Joyce pulled away from Sal and looked at Mrs. Mase and Micky. Sal rose and helped Jerry and Joyce stand. "We need to wash our hand's or Mom will not let us sit down to eat," said Sal smiling at the children. They hurried to wash their hands and Sal and Micky followed. Joyce looked surprised to see Sal and Micky going to wash their hands.

"I do not want to be sent away from the table," said Sal. "Me either," agreed Micky. Joyce laughed at the idea of anyone sending these big men away from the table for not washing their hands.

When Mrs. Mase realized what was going on, she inspected Sal and Micky's hands along with Jerry and Joyce's to be sure they were clean. When she pronounced them passable, the children laughed out loud.

Sal and Micky grinned and took their seats. It was nice to hear the children's laughter.

After eating, Sal called Brenda and gave her the information he had on the children. He did not want to go in and talk to Alex before he had a chance to talk to Selma about Jerry and Joyce. He needed to know how Selma felt before asking Alex for his help.

Suzy called Alex and arranged for Trey to meet her at the Marks' foster home in an hour. Alex relayed the message to Trey. Alex gave Trey, who was at home having lunch with his wife and daughter, the address and reminded him to keep him updated. Trey agreed and, after giving Lori and Crystal a hug and kiss, he left to meet Suzy. Trey arrived and had a short wait for Suzy.

Suzy greeted Trey and thanked him for coming along with them. "This is Belinda Frank, she is the worker in charge of the Marks' foster home," said Suzy. "Belinda, this is Trey Loden. He is an associate and is coming along for this visit."

"Pleased to meet you," said Trey holding out his hand to Belinda.

Belinda, reluctantly, accepted his handshake. Trey looked at Belinda sharply, but did not say anything. Suzy had been watching them closely. She looked startled at Trey's reaction, but she didn't say anything. Suzy turned and led the way to the Marks' front door.

Mrs. Marks opened the door at Suzy's knock. She had a small child in her arms. She looked surprised to see them, but opened the door wide and invited them in. They could hear the television in the living room and when Mrs. Marks led the way into the room, they found Mr. Marks. He was watching the television and answering the questions on the game show. He looked up. When he saw Belinda, he looked panicked for a minute, then put on a poker face when Belinda shook her head slightly.

Trey had been watching them intently. He did not miss the interaction between the two. Suzy was talking to Mrs. Marks, so Trey turned his attention to them.

I came by to let you know about the two young children, from your home, who were rescued from the child traffickers last night," said Suzy.

Mrs. Marks looked confused. "What children? We are not missing any children," she said.

Suzy looked startled. "The two young girls, Kay and Pam," said Suzy.

Mrs. Marks looked at her husband. Then she glanced at Belinda. "They were picked up last week. I was told they had been placed in permanent homes," said Mrs. Marks.

"Who picked up the girls, Mrs. Marks?" asked Suzy.

Mrs. Marks glanced at her husband again. "You told me Mrs. Frank picked up the children," she said.

Mr. Marks nodded. "She did." He agreed.

Belinda Frank glared at him. "You are not going to lay this on me," she said.

Suzy looked at Belinda. "How did the girls end up with the child traffickers?" she asked.

Trey stepped forward. "These two sold them. Belinda had the

connections and Mr. Marks has been supplying her with children. They have been splitting the money for the sale of the children," he concluded.

Mr. Marks and Belinda were both loudly protesting Trey's words. Suzy and Mrs. Marks were standing still, watching Belinda and Mr. Marks hurl accusations at each other. Mrs. Marks had tears running down her face. Suzy looked disgusted. She took out her phone and called 911.

When the other two realized she was calling the law, they started to try and run away. Trey stood in front of them and held up his hand. "Sit down," he said.

Belinda and Mr. Marks turned and sat down and stared at Trey. Trey stood in front of them. "When the police get here, you are going to tell them the truth. You are going to accept your punishment and never do anything to hurt or endanger children again. Neither of you will ever accept a job around children again," said Trey.

Trey looked around at Suzy. She was grinning at him. "Thanks," she said. How did you know?" she asked. "Their guardian angels told me they are brother and sister and have been working this scheme for a long time."

Suzy shook her head and looked at Belinda in disgust. "We are going to have to start screening our workers better," she said. Suzy turned to Mrs. Marks. When she saw her still crying, Suzy went over and put an arm around her. "I'm sorry. I know this is a bad time, but we are going to have to go over all the placements to your home. We have to see how many children have been sold to the traffickers."

Mrs. Marks nodded. "I understand." She raised tear drenched eyes to Suzy. "I only wanted to help the children," she whispered.

"She is telling the truth," said Trey. "She did not know what her husband was doing. She really only wants to help the children."

Suzy smiled at Trey and went to open the door for the police. Suzy explained why the police had been called. She waited while the police questioned Belinda and Mr. Marks. They both admitted their wrong- doing. The police took the two into custody to be charged down at the police station. Suzy agreed she would be down to press charges and watched as the police left with Belinda and Mr. Marks in handcuffs.

When they were gone, Suzy turned to Mrs. Marks. "I am not closing your foster home today, but I will be keeping a close eye on everything. I will be assigning a new worker to you, soon. In the meantime, I will be visiting you myself," said Suzy.

"Thank you," said Mrs. Marks.

"You do know we cannot have your husband involved with the foster home. He will be in prison for some time, but when he is released, if he returns here, we will have to close the foster home," said Suzy.

"I understand," said Mrs. Marks. "I will think about everything that has happened before I do anything."

"Okay," agreed Suzy.

When Trey and Suzy were outside, Trey looked at Suzy. "I wonder if I could get you to check on another child." When Suzy started to speak, Trey interrupted. "I know this child is not in the system. He was one of the children rescued from the child traffickers. When his mother picked him up at the hospital last night, he did not want to go with her. He clung to the policeman. The SWAT team was concerned about him. I have his name and address and I thought I would stand a better chance of getting in to see the child if you were with me," said Trey.

Suzy laughed. "You don't have to give me a hard sell," she said. "I will be glad to check on him. Do you want to go now?" she asked.

Trey's phone rand before he could answer. He glanced at the screen and saw Brenda's name, "Hello, Brenda," Trey answered.

"Hello, Trey, I am calling about the little boy from last night. Sal asked me to check him out. His name is Will Varnes. His mother is Hazel. His father is Jonah. His parents are divorced. The mother has custody. She does everything she can to keep the father from seeing Will. I called Mr. Varnes and asked him if he would be interested in custody. His answer was a firm "Yes." "He had not been told about

Will being missing. He was upset with his ex-wife for not telling him about his son's abduction. If you are going to see the boy, Have the father meet you there with his lawyer. I have a feeling you will need both," said Brenda.

"Thanks, Brenda, I was just about to go over there. Suzy Hamilton is going with me. Could you call Mr. Varnes and have him and his lawyer meet us there?" asked Trey

"Okay, good luck. If you need anything else, call me," said Brenda.

Trey looked at Suzy, who had been waiting patiently.

"Brenda said that Mrs. Varnes is divorced and tries to keep the father from seeing Will. She did not inform Mr. Varnes about Will's abduction. If you are ready, we can go and see what is going on with the Varnes family," said Trey.

"I'm ready," said Suzy. "I'll follow you."

They entered their cars and put the address in their GPS. Trey led the way to check on young Will Varnes.

Trey pulled to a stop in the Varnes driveway. Suzy pulled in behind him, as they started to the door, a car stopped at the curb. Two men exited the car and walked toward them. Trey and Suzy waited for them.

"You must be Mr. Varnes," said Suzy holding out a hand to shake. "I'm Suzy Hamilton from Child Protective Services and my associate is Trey Loden."

"Hello, Mrs. Hamilton, Mr. Loden." He clasped their hands in firm handshakes. "This is my lawyer Morris Kelp."

Mr. Kelp greeted them and shook their hands.

"Let's go inside and check on Will," said Suzy.

She turned and made her way to the front door with the three gentlemen following her.

Hazel Varnes opened the door at the knock but started to close it when she saw Jonah.

Trey put a hand on the door to stop it from closing.

"Mrs. Varnes, I am Suzy Hamilton. I am with Child Protective

Services. I am here to check on Will. We have to make sure he is alright after his ordeal," said Suzy.

Hazel stood back and let them enter. "Do I have to let him in?" asked Hazel motioning at Jonah.

"Yes, you do. We called Mr. Varnes and were surprised to find he did not know his son had been missing," said Suzy.

"I don't have to tell him anything. I have total custody," said Hazel.

"That is not correct, Mrs. Varnes. He is Will's father. He has to be told when something happens to his son," said Suzy. "Where is Will. I need to talk to him."

"I'll get him. He is in his room," said Hazel.

Hazel left the room and Suzy looked at Trey. Trey shook his head and sighed. Suzy looked disappointed.

They heard Hazel and Will coming. Hazel was berating Will as they entered. When Will spotted his father, He squealed "Dad" and, smiling big, Will ran to him. Jonah knelt and caught Will in his arms to hug him close.

"Are you alright, Buddy?" asked Jonah.

Will hugged his dad tighter. "You won't let Mom give me to the bad men again," begged Will.

Jonah focused stunned eyes on Hazel. "I promise, your mom is never going to give you to the bad men again," said Jonah.

"He's got it all wrong. I don't know why he thinks I gave him to anyone," protested Hazel. "You can't promise him anything. You have no say in what happens to him."

"You are wrong, Mrs. Varnes," said Suzy. "If what Will is saying is true, we will remove him from your custody."

"You can't prove anything. He is only four. You can't take his word over mine," said Hazel.

"She can take my word," said Trey. Everyone looked at Trey. "You are right. You didn't give Will to anyone. You sold him. You are going to sign the papers Jonah's lawyer has drawn, giving full custody to Jonah. The papers will specify there will be no visiting rights for you. If you do not sign, I will see that you are prosecuted and sent to jail for a long time. When your fellow prisoners find out what you did to Will, you will not have an easy time there."

Trey turned and stared at Hazel, waiting for her to speak. Hazel looked around at everyone looking at her in disgust. "Alright, I'll sign the papers. I only kept the brat to keep Jonah from getting him. Good riddance," she said.

Mr. Kelp opened his briefcase and withdrew the custody papers for her to sign. When she had signed, Suzy withdrew her notary stamp from her satchel and notarized the papers. Trey and Suzy signed as witnesses.

"Do you want to get his things?" Trey asked Jonah.

Jonah shook his head. "I will buy him new things. I just want to get out of here."

Mr. Kelp took the custody papers and started for the door. "I'll have these filed at the courthouse," he said. "If you have any problems, call me."

"I will, thank you," said Jonah. Taking Will, still held close in his arms, Jonah thanked Suzy and Trey and followed Mr. Kelp from the house.

Trey and Suzy turned to face Hazel. Hazel glared at them. "If you try to back out," said Trey. "I have the entire discussion recorded. It would be my pleasure to have you arrested."

Suzy and Trey turned and left. When they were outside the door, they heard something heavy hit the wall. They grinned at each other. "Someone is not too happy," said Trey with satisfaction.

Suzy laughed. "I love working with you guys from Avorn. You sure keep things interesting," said Suzy.

Trey smiled and started guiding Suzy to her car and opening her door for her. "Thank you for helping us with Will," he said.

"It was my pleasure," said Suzy. She started her car and backed out of the drive. With a wave she drove away, and Trey went to his car to follow. He had quite a tale to relate to Alex. He also wanted to have Brenda make a copy of the recording and place it in the safe at

Avorn building. If it was ever needed it would be safe and easy to produce.

Sal and Micky had taken the names and addresses of the three other children picked up from the hospital by their parents. They drove to the homes, one at a time, and checked on the children. The children had told their parents about being rescued by Sal. He tried to tell the parents it was a team effort, but they insisted on thanking him. The children were doing great. They were clinging close to their parents but were happy to be home.

When Sal and Micky left the third home, they were satisfied the children were happy and safe. They were convinced the parents would keep a closer eye on the children in the future, and the children would stay close and not wander away.

"Should we go by and tell Alex the children are okay?" asked Micky

"I'll call Brenda and have her pass a message to him. I don't want to talk to him until I have a chance to talk to Selma," said Sal.

"Okay," Micky nodded his understanding.

"It is almost time for school to be out, why don't we go there and wait for Selma and Stacy?" asked Micky.

Sal grinned. "Maybe I can decide how to approach Selma about adopting Jerry and Joyce," commented Sal.

CHAPTER 14

"Hi, Micky and I are outside waiting for our favorite ladies," thought Sal to Selma.

"We will be out soon. Stacy and I were dismissed from classes early. We were helping make plans for decorating the gym for the prom. I love you," thought Selma.

"I love you, too," thought Sal.

Sal leaned back in his seat with a sigh. "Selma and Stacy will be here soon. They are helping make plans for the prom," said Sal.

Micky grinned. He was anxious to see Stacy. Sometimes it felt like he was dreaming. It was hard to believe he had found his one true love. He was anxious to start their future together. Micky sighed. He realized Stacy needed time to learn more about him, but the waiting was hard. He was ready to start the future, promised him by his guardian angel and the magic mirror.

Sal had been sitting quietly thinking about how to approach Selma about Jerry and Joyce. He wanted to present his need to help them without making Selma think she had to do what he wanted. He wanted her to be happy with the arrangement, too.

The girls exited the door together. Sal and Micky left the car when they saw Selma, and then Stacy coming through the door. Micky took Stacy's hand and guided her to the back seat. He entered the back seat beside her and closed the door before pulling her close for a quick kiss.

Sal guided Selma to the front passenger door, but before he seated her, he gave her a quick kiss. "I know," said Sal when Selma started to protest. She looked around to see if anyone was watching them. "I couldn't wait," said Sal. He helped her into the car and went to the driver's seat.

"Micky is it okay if we go by our apartment and get your car so you can take Stacy home?" asked Sal.

"Okay," agreed Micky

"I don't mind," said Stacy. "I do have to go home before you guys are called out on a case. I don't have any clothes with me, and I can't keep borrowing from Selma."

They all laughed. "I don't mind you borrowing my clothes," said Selma.

"I know, thanks," said Stacy.

"You look beautiful," said Micky softly.

Stacy smiled at Micky and squeezed his hand.

"We don't have any cases that can't wait," said Sal. He glanced at Selma. "I have something I need to talk to you about," he said.

"I need to talk to you about something, too," agreed Selma.

Sal glanced at her curiously. "Is something wrong?" he asked.

"No," said Selma. "I just have something I need to discuss with you."

Sal looked at her again. "Okay," he agreed.

Sal pulled to a stop in the apartment building parking lot beside Micky's car. They all got out and stood looking around. The girls were looking at the apartment building and the guys were looking at the girls.

"Would you girls like to come in for a minute for a drink?" asked Sal.

"Sure," said Selma and Stacy in agreement. They were both

curious to see the apartment where their guys lived. Sal took Selma's hand and led the way to the front door. Micky followed with Stacy's hand clasped tightly in his hand.

Sal unlocked the door and turned the light on. He looked around to see how big of a mess they had left the apartment in. It didn't look to bad, he thought.

"It's fine," said Selma entering behind him and edging him aside.

Sal flashed her a small smile. He had not realized he had sent his thoughts to Selma.

Stacy looked around. "You guys are very neat, You, should have seen my brother's room before he left for the Navy. It was always a disaster. It was a good thing mother had a cleaning lady. The cleaning lady would make sure everything was straightened before mother had a chance to see it.

Micky looked startled. "You have a cleaning lady?" he asked.

Stacy shook her head, "My mother has a cleaning lady. She does not have her clean my room. Mother did not know the cleaning lady cleaned my brother's room. Mother insisted she was not paying for us to be lazy. She said we could take care of ourselves. The cleaning lady had a sweet spot for my brother. After she heard mother yelling at him for his messy room, she started slipping in and straightening for him," concluded Stacy with a smile.

Micky looked at her blankly for a minute, then smiled. "Did you want a drink before we go?" he asked. Micky looked around and saw he and Stacy were alone. Sal and Selma had gone to the kitchen.

Stacy shook her head. "I didn't really want a drink. I just wanted to see your apartment. Are we in a hurry to leave?" she asked.

"No," said Micky with a grin. "I think Sal and Selma want to talk about something, but they can talk in the kitchen," said Micky.

"Good," said Stacy moving closer to Micky and gazing in his eyes. "I'm not in a hurry to go home as long as you guys are not going to be called out."

Micky put his arms around her and pulled her close for a kiss. The kiss became intense very quickly. They were both very into it.

Sal had started to go back into the front room to see if Stacy wanted a drink. When he saw what was happening, he pulled back into the kitchen and joined Selma seated on a bar stool.

Sal sat on the stool next to Selma and took her hand. "You said there was something you wanted to talk about," said Sal.

Selma nodded. She looked like she didn't know where to start.

"What is it?" asked Sal gently.

"It's about Jerry and Joyce," said Selma.

Sal stiffened and looked at her sharply. "What about them?" he asked.

"I was wondering if there was any way we could help them, maybe give them a home. I know we are not married, yet. I don't even know if you want to take them, but it breaks my heart to think of them being put in the system again," said Selma. She raised tear drenched eyes to Sal.

Sal leaned in and kissed her. "You are amazing," he said. "I was going to talk to you about them. I wasn't sure how you would feel about having to start our life together with a ready- made family."

Selma kissed him back. "I am used to having children around. It would be selfish of me to not want to help these youngsters when they need us so badly. Do you think we could get custody or adopt them?" asked Selma.

Sal looked at her and shook his head. "I don't know. I think Alex will be able to help. He asked me if I wanted anything permanent. I told him I had to discuss it with you first. I'll have to talk to him and see what he can arrange," explained Sal. "We may have to move up our marriage plans. We may not be able to get the children until we are married."

Selma brightened when Sal said he had told Alex he had to talk to her first. She loved him putting her feelings first. It made her feel closer to him.

"We can have a civil ceremony and have a church one later," said Selma.

"What about your college?" asked Sal.

"I can take some classes online. If I need to go the college for some classes, we will work that out later," declared Selma.

Sal pulled her close and kissed her. "I love you. I am so happy our guardian angels and the magic mirror agreed we are a match. Every dilemma can be solved if love is factored in," whispered Sal.

Selma nodded her agreement. She remembered her guardian angel had made a similar remark. It made a lot more sense when Sal said it. Selma stopped thinking and started enjoying the feelings Sal stirred in her.

After a satisfactory intermission, Micky and Stacy made their way to the kitchen. Sal and Selma were sitting at the table. Selma was sitting in Sal's lap. Stacy grinned at Selma. "You look comfortable," she remarked.

Selma smiled and flashed Sal a smoldering look. "I am. I have the best seat in the apartment," she declared.

Stacy and Micky laughed. Sal smiled and nuzzled her cheek.

"Have you two worked things out?" asked Micky.

"Yes," said Sal. "Selma and I are going to talk to Alex and see if he can help us adopt Jerry and Joyce."

Stacy looked at Selma. "I know you were worrying about them. I hope it all works out for you," she said going forward and giving Selma a hug.

"Thank you," said Selma. "We will make it work out. I am sure there is a way. If one way doesn't work, we will try another way."

"What do you mean?" asked Sal looking at Selma.

"I am a citizen of Cendera. My Great Grandfather is one of the founders. If we were to be married in Cendera. A local judge would let us adopt Jerry and Joyce. It would be legal in all states. There is no way a judge in Cendera could say no to a founding family's request," said Selma.

"Wow," said Micky. "It would be great to pay another visit to Cendera."

Sal gave Micky a stern look. "We have to give Alex a chance first. He may be able to arrange everything," said Sal.

"I know," agreed Micky with a nod. "I just thought it would be a cool trip. I bet the kids would love it."

"Don't you say anything to anyone about a trip to Cendera before I get a chance to talk to Alex. I don't want to have anyone disappointed," said Sal'

"I'm sorry I brought it up," said Selma. "I was just trying to help."

Sal hugged her. "It's okay. If we can't figure a way to resolve things here, we will see about Cendera," promised Sal.

Micky tugged on Stacy's hand. "Would you like to get something to eat before I take you home?" asked Micky.

"Sure, are you guys going to join us?" she asked Sal and Selma.

Sal shook his head. "Selma and I are going to make a quick trip to Avorn Building and talk to Alex. I want to see what plans he has for adopting Jerry and Joyce," said Sal.

Selma stood and pulled on Sal's hand. "Let's go. I want to hear what he has to say," said Selma.

They left the apartment. Micky and Stacy drove away in Micky's car with a quick wave at Selma and Sal. Sal helped Selma into his car and turned to go to Avorn Building. He was anxious to talk to Alex.

"Maybe you should check and see if Alex is in before going," said Selma.

Sal grinned at Selma. "Good idea," he said.

He dialed Lynn. "Hello, Lynn. Is Alex still in the office?" he asked.

"Yes, are you on your way in?" asked Lynn.

"Yes, I have Selma with me. We wanted to talk to Alex. Would you let him know we are on our way?" he asked.

"Sure," agreed Lynn. "See you soon." She hung up the phone and punched in Alex's number.

"Yes, Lynn," said Alex.

"Sal and Selma are on their way in to see you. They will be here soon," said Lynn.

"Okay," agreed Alex. "Send them in when they get here," said Alex.

He hung up the phone and looked at Trey. "It seems Sal has talked to Selma about the children he carried to his mother. They are on their way in," said Alex.

Trey grinned. "Are you going to be able to help then adopt the children?" asked Trey.

"I have already talked to Judge Parks. He said he didn't see any problem with them adopting. He did say they needed to be married first. I told him Sal is having a house built. He was okay with them staying with Mr. and Mrs. Mase until the house is built," said Alex.

Trey laughed. "You are always a step ahead," said Trey.

Alex smiled. "Those children need to be in a settled environment quickly. They have been tossed around enough," said Alex.

"I agree," said Trey soberly. "I had better go so you can talk to Sal and Selma. Let me know if I can help," said Trey.

"I will, Thanks for taking care of the situations with the children," said Alex.

Trey grinned. "Believe me, it was my pleasure," said Trey with a laugh as he left.

Trey waved at Lynn as he passed her desk. He met Sal and Selma at the elevator.

"Hi, Trey," said Sal. "Do you know Selma Dolan?"

"Hello Sal. It's nice to meet you Miss Dolan. Alex is waiting on you. Good luck with the children," said Trey. He entered the elevator and was gone.

Sal smiled at Selma. Trey and his wife are great agents and they are very close friends with Alex and Mariam," explained Sal leading Selma to Lynn's desk.

"Hi, Lynn, this is Selma Dolan. We are here to see Alex."

"Hello, Miss Dolan. Alex said for you to come right in," said Lynn with a smile for them.

Selma smiled and greeted Lynn as Sal lad her to Alex's office.

Alex rose when they entered. "Hello, Selma, has Sal convinced you to adopt the children?" asked Alex.

Selma grinned. "Hello Mr. Avorn. Actually, I convinced Sal we needed to adopt Jerry and Joyce," said Selma with a smile and a glance at Sal.

Sal smiled and nodded. "Selma asked me about us adopting before I could ask her," said Sal'

Alex grinned. "I'm glad you are in agreement," he said. "I talked to Judge Parks. He doesn't see any problem with you adopting the two children. He did say you needed to be married before you file for adoption. I explained about you building a house in Avorn Acres. Judge Parks said It would be okay if you lived with your folks, temporary, until your house is ready. You need to discuss it with them and be sure they are okay with you all living there with them for a couple of months. We need to know before we file. If they are not agreeable, we can make other arrangements. You could move into one of the apartments on the sixth floor." Alex paused to let them absorb what he had told them.

"I'm sure my parents will be okay with us staying with them, but I will talk to them first. Selma suggested we have a civil ceremony before we file and have a church ceremony later," said Sal.

Alex shook his head. "There is no need to have two ceremonies. Selma has prom this week. She has graduation next week. If you reserve the church for the weekend after the graduation, it will give me time to arrange for your aunt's family to come and give you time to get ready. I will explain everything to Judge Parks. He can have the papers ready. We can go in and let him sign everything along with you and Selma. I will be signing as your sponsor. I'll arrange for us to meet with the judge a couple of days after the wedding. Does that sound alright to you?" asked Alex.

Sal and Selma were beaming. They nodded, enthusiastically.

"It sounds perfect," said Selma.

"How did you make all of these arrangements so fast?" asked Sal. "I hadn't agreed to adopt the children."

Alex smiled. "I could see you had your heart set on keeping the children. I wanted to be ready when you came to see me," said Alex.

"Thank you," said Selma. "How did you know I wanted my aunt's family here for the wedding?"

"I promised your aunt to let her know how you were doing. I knew she would want to be at your wedding," said Alex. "Is there anything else I can help you with?" asked Alex.

"There is one more thing," said Selma.

Sal and Alex looked at her inquiringly. "What do you need?" asked Alex.

"You are my guardian, aren't you?" asked Selma.

Alex nodded. "Yes, I am," he agreed.

"I was wondering if you would give me away at the wedding?" asked Selma.

Alex looked startled. "I would be honored," he said. Alex sat back and smiled. "I'm glad you are having the wedding soon. Mariam is going to want to attend. She is seven months now. We wouldn't want her to get any closer to delivery before the wedding."

Selma smiled. "It would make for a memorable wedding," she laughed.

"It is one memory I would just as soon not have to deal with," said Alex. "I will talk to Judge Parks and fill him in and start everything in motion. I will let you know what he says. He may want to meet with you and the children before he does the paperwork."

"Okay let us know what he says," agreed Sal, rising from his chair. He helped Selma to stand and Alex rose and walked them out.

"Everything will work out. Any dilemma can be solved with love," said Alex as the elevator door slid shut between them.

"I keep hearing that phrase," said Selma.

"What phrase?" asked Sal.

"About love being the answer to any dilemma. First my guardian angel used it. Then you said it, and now, Alex said it," said Selma.

"Well," shrugged Sal. "If your guardian angel agrees, I guess it must be true."

CHAPTER 15

*W*hen Micky and Stacy pulled up to the gate of the gated subdivision where her mother's house was located, Stacy entered the code to open the gate so they could enter.

"Will I need a code to get out?" asked Micky as he drove through the gate.

Stacy shook her head and smiled. "No, the gate opens automatically when approached from inside. You only need a code to get in. You can also call on the intercom and have the home- owner open the gate for you."

"I like Avorn Acres setup better. The guards will know who is entering and can call for help if it is needed," observed Micky.

Micky looked around at the houses as they drove to and parked in the Clark driveway. It was a typical rich man's neighborhood. The lawns were neat and looked like they had all been designed by the same person. He could see yard workers cutting grass and trimming hedges.

Micky stopped the car in the driveway and went around to open Stacy's door and help her out. Stacy led the way to the door. She had a key in one hand and was holding tightly to Micky with the other.

After Stacy unlocked the door, they entered the front hallway. Pulling Micky along with her, Stacy went into the living room. Micky looked around curiously. The room was expensively furnished, but it was not to Micky's taste. He preferred a more homey atmosphere.

Stacy, watching Micky's face, smiled at his reaction. "Our house is much, nicer and we can furnish however we are comfortable with," she promised.

Micky smiled and kissed her. "You said 'our' house," he said smiling.

Stacy nodded. "We are going to be married. It is our house."

"Oh, yes," said Micky kissing her again.

The front door opened, and Mavis Clark breezed into the room. She stopped short when she saw Stacy in Micky's arms,

"Really, Stacy," Mavis sneered. "Is this what you have come to?" demanded Mavis.

Micky and Stacy both stiffened. "Mother," said Stacy. "This is Micky Ansel. He and I are engaged."

Mavis shook her head. "No way am I going let you upset my campaign by showing up with this hoodlum," declared Mavis.

"Micky is not a hoodlum. He is a security agent, and you do not have to worry about your campaign. I have no intention of helping you with your campaign. I will be busy getting married," declared Stacy.

Micky, gently, turned Stacy to face him. "Go and get what things you want to take with you. I'll wait here," he said.

"What things?" demanded Mavis. "You are not taking anything I have bought."

"You did not by my things, Mother. I worked and bought my own clothes and anything else in my room. I even paid for my furniture. I am just taking clothes and jewelry tonight, but I will be sending for my other things. You had better not give me a problem with my things. If you try to stop me, I will be sure the press finds out and you can kiss your office goodbye," said Stacy.

Stacy left the room after giving Micky's hand a squeeze. She hurried to her room to pack as many clothes as she could fit in her large suitcase. It felt good to stand up to her mother, for a change, she thought.

Mavis looked at Micky. "You have turned my daughter against me," she accused.

Micky shook his head. "No, you did it all on your own." Micky looked at her hard. "Alex told us you were a hard ass, but I had no idea how bad you really were," stated Micky.

Mavis looked stunned. She couldn't believe anyone would talk to her the way this man did. "Do you know who I am?" she asked.

"Yes," said Micky. "You are the district attorney. You are also the one who took credit for saving the children SWAT and Avorn agents pulled out of the basement last night," said Micky.

Mavis paled. "How did you know about those children?" she asked.

"I know about them, because I was one of the Avorn agents pulling them to safety last night," said Micky.

"You work for Alex Avorn," said Mavis faintly.

Micky nodded. He turned to Stacy as she entered the room and hurried to take the large suitcase she brought into the room. Neither Stacy nor Micky said anything to Mavis as they left. Mavis was sitting in a chair looking stunned.

Micky put Stacy's suitcase in the trunk of his car and helped Stacy into the front passenger seat. They left without looking back. They were glad to leave the neighborhood behind them.

Sal and Selma went to the Mase home to talk to Jerry, Joyce, and Mr. and Mrs. Mase. They wanted to be sure the children wanted to be a part of their family. They also had to talk to Mr. and Mrs. Mase about living with them until their new house was finished.

Selma smiled at Sal and squeezed his hand. She was sitting as close to him as the seat belt would let her. Selma lay her cheek against Sal's shoulder and rubbed it back and forth. "I love you," said Selma.

Sal glanced down at her. "I love you, too," he said. "I never thought I could love anyone as much as I love you. You are my other half," said Sal.

Selma looked up at him with tears in her eyes.

"I did not mean to make you cry," said Sal.

"They are happy tears. What you said was so beautiful. I have been waiting for you my entire life. Having your love and having a chance to adopt Jerry and Joyce is a dream come true. I know everything is going to work for us. We will make it work. My guardian angel says I have nothing to worry about. She said everything is as it should be," said Selma.

Sal took her hand and placed it on his leg with his hand holding it in place. "If your guardian angel is on our side, we have it made," Sal said with a smile.

Sal pulled into the Mase driveway and stopped the car. He pulled Selma close and kissed her before helping her from the car and leading the way inside.

Mr. Mase was sitting at the table reading the paper. Mrs. Mase was standing at the stove stirring a pan of spaghetti sauce.

Sal went over and kissed his mom on the cheek. "Where are Jerry and Joyce?" he asked.

They are in the living room," said Mrs. Mase. "I found some old games you boys played when you were younger. They are having fun with them."

"Selma and I will go and talk to them. After we talk to them, we need to talk to you and Dad. I think Alex has found a way for us to adopt them, but we have to talk to them first and be sure it's what they want," said Sal.

Mrs. Mase smiled, and Mr. Mase looked up from his paper. "We will be right here," he said. "Good luck."

"Thanks," said Sal. Selma just smiled nervously and holding tight to Sal's hand accompanied him to the living room.

Jerry and Joyce looked up with big smiles when Sal and Selma entered the room. Joyce hurried over to give, first Selma and then Sal, a hug. Jerry stood and looked like he wanted to join them but was embarrassed after his earlier emotions.

Sal smiled and held up his arm in invitation. Jerry hurried to join in the hugging.

"We need to talk to both of you," said Selma leading the way to the sofa. She tugged Joyce's hand and pulled her down beside her on the sofa. Sal seated himself and Jerry beside them. Jerry and Joyce stared at Selma wide eyed but did not say anything.

Selma cleared her throat nervously and glanced at Sal for help. Sal smiled. "We were wondering how the two of you would feel about being a part of our family. Selma and I are going to be married, and we would love to adopt you and make you our children," said Sal.

Jerry and Joyce were smiling through tears. "Are you really going to adopt us?" whispered Joyce.

"If it is okay with you," said Selma gently hugging the young girl close.

Sal smiled at Jerry. "Would you be okay with us adopting you and Joyce?" he asked.

Jerry nodded. "It would be great," he said. "Would we change our last name to Mase?"

Sal laughed, "Yes you would. It will be a couple of weeks before we can go before the judge and finalize the adoption. The judge may want to talk to you and Joyce. He will want to be sure you are okay with the adoption." finished Sal.

"I'll tell him 'yes,'" said Joyce who had been listening to Sal and Jerry's conversation.

Selma and Sal smiled at her enthusiasm. Jerry smiled also. "I'll tell him 'yes,' too," he agreed. "Where are we going to live?" asked Jerry.

"We are working on living arrangements," said Sal. "Our new home is being built. I'll take you both out to see where we will be living, soon. It will be a couple of months before it will be ready. We will have to discuss our living arrangements before we can decide on where we will live."

Jerry and Joyce nodded happily. They were perfectly happy to let Sal and Selma deal with the details.

They all looked around as Mr. and Mrs. Mase joined them in the living room. Mr. Mase smiled at the ecstatic looks on the faces of the children, and the happy faces of Sal and Selma.

"We are going to be adopted," said Joyce happily. "We are going to be Mases., too."

"You are?" said Mr. Mase smiling. Joyce nodded. "Well, welcome to the family. Come and give your granddad a hug." He held his arms open and Joyce ran over and hugged him. When Joyce turned him loose, she turned and went into Mrs. Mase's arms to receive a hug from her. Mr. Mase held open his arms to Jerry. Jerry shyly went over and joined the hug fest.

Smiling, Sal and Selma sat on the sofa. It was great to have the approval of his parents, thought Sal. Mr. and Mrs. Mase came over and congratulated Selma and Sal. Sal could tell they were happy about the adoption.

"What did you want to talk to us about?" asked Mr. Mase after he sat in a chair facing the sofa. Mrs. Mase sat in another chair and Jerry and Joyce joined Sal and Selma on the sofa.

Selma put an arm around Joyce and held Sal's hand with her other hand. "Alex arranged for Judge Parks to approve the adoption, but he won't approve it until we are married. He also wants to talk with us and both children. Well, Selma's prom is this next Friday, her graduation is the next Tuesday. Alex said for us to talk to the church officials and see if we can have the church the following weekend. While we make wedding arrangements, he will make arrange for Selma's aunt and her family to be here for the wedding. We can meet with the judge the Monday after the wedding and he will sign the final adoption papers. The only problem is our house will not be ready for a couple of months. I was wondering if we could stay on here until the house is ready. If you don't think it will be, too crowded," concluded Sal.

Mrs. Mase scoffed. "Too crowded. We will be using the same rooms we are using now. You will move into Selma's room. The only thing different is we would set an extra plate on the table at meals. You are here so much, we already set your plate," she said.

Everyone laughed at her words. After all it was true, Sal and Micky did stop by at mealtime often.

"You are always welcome here. It has been a pleasure to have young people in the house again. You all can stay as long as you need to," confirmed Mr. Mase.

Sal went and hugged his dad and then his mom. Selma hugged them, also. "Thank you," said Selma smiling happily at her new family'

"Well," said Mrs. Mase. "Let's eat some spaghetti."

Everyone headed for the kitchen. As they passed into the hall the doorbell sounded. Mr. Mase opened the door for Micky and Stacy. "Come on in," he invited. "You are just in time for spaghetti."

Micky and Stacy joined them and followed them to the table.

"Oh, one of my favorite meals," said Stacy beaming at Mrs. Mase while Micky held her chair and seated her at the table.

Selma quickly placed two more plates and utensils on the table before she allowed Sal to seat her.

Selma looked at Stacy curiously after they said the blessing and began to eat. "I thought Micky was taking you home," Selma remarked.

"He did," agreed Stacy. "My mother came in before Micky left. She called Micky a hoodlum and forbid me to marry him, so I packed my clothes and left." Stacy glanced at Mrs. Mase. "I was hoping I could stay here a few days, until Micky and I can be married."

Mrs. Mase smiled. "You are welcome to stay as long as you like. When are you and Micky planning to be married?"

"When we can arrange a ceremony," said Micky.

"Sal and Selma are planning to be married the weekend after

graduation, if they can reserve the church. Why don't you have a double wedding?" suggested Mr. Mase.

"That's a great idea, Dad. Stacy can stay here until the wedding, and she and Micky will have the apartment to themselves afterwards." Sal looked at Micky. "I will continue to pay my share of the bills for a couple of months until our houses are ready to move into,"

"You and Selma don't mind sharing your wedding day?" Micky asked.

"It will make it more special," said Selma. "I would love having Stacy with me."

Selma turned to Stacy. "Joyce can move in with me, and you can have her room. You will have more privacy and I can get better acquainted with my daughter."

Joyce beamed at Selma. "Joyce won't mind, will you?" asked Selma. Joyce shook her head and smiled at everyone.

"Thanks," said Stacy. She gave Joyce a thumbs up and a smile. Joyce returned her thumbs up.

Micky turned to Sal. "Alex was able to arrange for you and Selma to adopt Jerry and Joyce?" he asked.

"Yes, he talked to Judge Parks and arranged everything. We can't sign the adoption papers until after the wedding, but it is arranged," confirmed Sal.

"Congratulations, to all of you," said Micky. "I know you and Selma will make great parents."

"Do we have to go back to school since we are being adopted?" asked Jerry. He was more interested in things affecting him and Joyce.

Everyone smiled at Jerry and Joyce. "School is almost out for the year," said Selma. "I think it would be better if you started fresh in the fall." Jerry's face brightened. "However. I will be tutoring you both this summer. You missed a bunch of classes. I wouldn't want you to fall behind." Jerry's face sobered then brightened again.

"I am glad you are tutoring us. We will study hard. We want to make you and Sal proud of us," said Jerry. Joyce nodded her agreement.

Selma rose and went around the table to the children. She knelt and put an arm around each. "We are already very proud of you both. I'm glad you are going to study hard, but you do not have to earn our love or our pride in you. You already have it. We are proud to be your parents. Both children hugged her tight.

When Selma rose to go back to her seat to finish eating, she looked around and saw there were a lot of misty eyes around the table. When she sat in her chair beside Sal, he pulled her into a hug and gave her a quick kiss.

After starting to eat again, Selma glanced at Stacy. "Did you bring your prom dress?" asked Selma.

Stacy nodded. "What color is it?" asked Micky.

"It's soft rose," said Stacy with a smile. Micky nodded and stored the information away for later.

"We need to go on a shopping trip to the mall, tomorrow," said Sal. "Mom pointed out Jerry and Joyce are in desperate need of new clothes. I asked Alex for the day off. He said fine, if there are no emergencies. So, are you all up for a trip to the mall?" asked Sal.

"Oh, yes, I love shopping in the mall. Can we stop for pizza in the food court?" asked Selma.

"Sure," said Sal indulgently. "Mom do you want to go with us?" asked Sal.

Mrs. Mase looked around at all the excited faces and shrugged. "I think a trip to the mall is just what I need," she agreed.

"Will you come with us, Stacy? There is no school tomorrow. They dismissed classes so we could get ready for prom," said Selma.

"Okay," agreed Stacy. "Who can turn down shopping in the mall?" she asked.

They finished their meal, and Micky and Sal went to get Stacy's suitcase and take it upstairs while Selma, Stacy and Joyce cleared the table and put the dishes in the dishwasher. Jerry accompanied Mr.

and Mrs. Mase to the living room. He and Mr. Mase were busy talking and getting to know each other as family.

When they all were together again in the living room, Sal asked Mrs. Mase if there was someone she could call to see if the church was free when they wanted it. She went to get her list of names from church and called the church secretary. The secretary checked her list and found the church was free when they needed it. Mrs. Mase explained about the double wedding asked her to reserve it for them. She promised Selma and Sal along with Micky and Stacy would be by to talk to the pastor about the ceremony before the date of the wedding.

When she hung up the phone, Sal gave her a hug, then hugged Selma. "One step closer," he declared. "Yes," Selma happily agreed. They looked over at Micky and Stacy who were celebrating the news in their own way.

"Are you going to take two cars?" asked Mr. Mase.

"No," said Sal. "I asked Alex if we could borrow the limo for out shopping trip and for the prom the next night, He said it was fine. I think he is enjoying the situation as much as we are. Alex loves to be in the middle of things. He is staying close to home more because of Mariam's pregnancy. I think this gives him something else to think about. I'm sure Mariam would thank us for distracting him," laughed Sal.

Everyone smiled at the thought of anyone distracting Alex Avorn. He was always very aware of everything going on around him.

The shopping trip went smoothly. Sal drove Micky in to pick up the Limo. At the mall the ladies led Joyce into a children's store for girls while Micky and Sal accompanied Jerry into a young man's store. After they loaded up with everything they agreed the children had to have, they met at the food court. There, they all indulged in different toppings on their slices of pizza.

They had one last stop after eating. They stopped at the toy store and indulged the children in several new miniature video games. The children were very excited. They could hardly wait to get home, change into their new play clothes and learn how to play their new games.

When they were back at the Mase house, everyone grabbed bags and started unloading. Jerry came down to the living room after dropping his things in his room. He found Sal there alone. Jerry stopped in front of Sal and looked at him seriously.

"You didn't have to buy us all of this stuff," said Jerry. "I am just happy to have someone really want me."

Sal pulled Jerry into his arms. We want you. We are not trying to buy your affection. We are mostly buying because it makes us feel good. We are having a great time becoming parents and we just want to share the joy. If we do anything you don't agree with. Talk to either me or Selma, and we will work it out. We may not always do things your way, but we will listen and talk it out, okay?" asked Sal.

Jerry nodded and, after one last hug, Sal released him. He returned to his room and to his new games.

CHAPTER 16

The next evening Sal and Micky were at the Mase house waiting for Selma and Stacy to make their appearance. Nelson was the limo's official driver for the night. He would stay with the limo and be sure it was protected from any pranksters while waiting for the prom to be over.

Sal looked up as Selma entered the living room. He drew a deep breath and smiled as he gazed at her. "You look beautiful," he said.

"Thank you," answered Selma with a grin.

"Gorgeous," whispered Micky as he gazed at Stacy, who entered behind Selma.

Both men came forward and presented their ladies with their corsages. "We just went into the flower shop and told the lady what color we wanted, and she went and found them for us," said Sal. While tying the sea green flowers on Selma's wrist

"Yeah," agreed Micky while working on Stacy's flower. "I would have never found soft rose if I had to pick it out," agreed Micky.

"It's beautiful," said Selma as she admired her first corsage. It was a perfect match for her dress.

"Yes, it is," agreed Stacy as she gave Micky a quick kiss in thanks.

"Alright," said Mrs. Mase. "Stand over here by the fireplace and let me get pictures."

They followed her instructions, and she soon had many pictures taken. She took some of each couple and some of all four together. She even included some of Sal and Selma with Jerry and Joyce. The two children were having a great time watching the couples prepare for the dance.

"You have enough pictures," complained Sal. We have to go, or we will be late for the dance,"

"Brenda called me, and I promised I would take lots of pictures and send her copies on the computer," explained Mrs. Mase with a smile of satisfaction. "I think I have some good shots," she said. "Jerry is going to help me send them to Brenda."

Sal gave Jerry a thumbs up, and Jerry smiled proudly.

"They will be fine," said Sal. He quickly led the way out before she could decide to take more pictures.

Nelson opened the back door of the limo for them when he saw them coming.

"You guys are lucky," declared Nelson grinning at Sal and Micky. "What did you ever do to deserve such beautiful ladies?"

"I don't know, but I am sure glad to say she's mine," agreed Micky helping Stacy into the car.

"Me, too," agreed Sal gazing at Selma.

"Hi, Nelson," said Selma. "Thanks for being our driver. Have you met Stacy?'

"No, it's nice to meet you, Stacy. Welcome to the Avorn family. Anytime you need us just call. We will do all we can to help," said Nelson smiling at Stacy.

"Thank you, it's nice to meet you. I think I lucked out when Micky and I became a couple," Stacy said as she felt Micky holding her close.

Nelson looked at Selma.

"Did you work out your problem with your dad?" Nelson asked Selma.

"I think so," said Selma. "I still have to arrange a visit with my brothers. There has been so much going on, I haven't had time to set up a meeting with them."

"We will get to it," said Sal. "But, now, we need to go to the dance."

Selma smiled at Sal and allowed herself to be seated for the drive to the dance.

Nelson was soon joining a group of limos dropping the decked-out seniors at their dance to celebrate their final year of high school.

They were walking toward the decorated gym, when Selma looked at Sal and grinned. "I don't think I have mentioned it, but you and Micky look great in those tuxes," said Selma squeezing his arm.

"You surely do," agreed Stacy gazing at Micky with a smile.

"Thank you. Micky and I rented them for two weeks so we would have them for the wedding," said Sal.

Selma stopped in her track's, a stunned look on her face. "We have to go shopping for our wedding dresses," she said.

"Not tonight," said Sal gently leading her on as Stacy and Micky laughed. "We will see about shopping tomorrow."

"Okay," agreed Selma somewhat reassured.

They handed their tickets to the person at the door, who happened to be Coach Lewis.

"Have a good time," said Coach Lewis waving them on in.

They walked through the door and stopped and stared. There were streamers everywhere. Some of the streamers had stars attached to them. In the stars were pictures of the graduating seniors. There were machines set around the room. The machines made it look like stars were coming out of the floor and rising to the ceiling. The banner over the stage had the word "OUR RISING STARS." There was a poster behind the banner with the pictures of the seniors.

"It's beautiful," whispered Selma. Stacy, Sal and Micky agreed.

The band was playing, so Sal and Micky drew the girls out onto the dance floor. Selma noticed some of the girls watching them and talking among themselves. She ignored them and let Sal pull her closer, as he led her through the dance.

The band went from one song to another without stopping, so they stayed on the floor and danced on. They had danced through about four songs when Selma decided to stop and get a drink. She and Sal made their way to the table with the punch bowl. When Sal went to get Selma a glass of punch, Becky a girl in Selma's math class, stood close to Selma and whispered.

"I saw Phillip Loris pour some alcohol in the punch," said Becky.

"Really," said Selma. "Doesn't he have a date?" asked Selma.

"No," said Becky shaking her head. "He came stag."

Selma looked at the punch bowl. She whispered a few words and made a circle with her fingers. "The punch looks fine," she said taking the glass Sal handed her. She sniffed her glass and handed it to Sal. "Would you taste this and see if alcohol has been added?" she asked.

Sal looked surprised but tasted the punch. "It's fine," he said. Selma smiled at Becky. "Phillip must have thought he added alcohol, but someone fooled him and changed it to water. Tell everyone the punch is fine. If you hear of anyone else trying to spike our punch, let me know."

Becky nodded and hurried away to spread the word the punch was okay.

Sal looked at Selma. "Someone spiked the punch?" he asked.

Selma nodded while she looked around trying to spot Phillip. "It's okay, now," she said absentmindedly.

Sal grinned. "What did you do to it?" he asked.

Selma smiled. "I neutralized the alcohol. It is plain water now," she said.

Sal just shook his head and stared at Selma with amusement.

"There is Phillip. Let's get a little closer," said Selma. Sal followed as Selma made her way closer to where Phillip was laughing and joking with his friends. Selma said a few words, softly, circled her fingers and watched Phillip double over in pain.

Some of his friends helped him out of the room. Coach Lewis had been watching Phillip, also. He had heard the rumors about the alcohol added to the punch. He saw Selma at the punch bowl and later watched her just before Phillip doubled over in pain. Coach Lewis made his way over to Selma and Sal.

Selma looked up to see Coach Lewis standing beside her and Sal. "Is he going to be alright?" asked Coach Lewis.

Selma looked at him in surprise. Coach Lewis smiled. "One of my cousins married a man from Cendera," said Coach Lewis.

Selma smiled. "He will be fine tomorrow. He just has a stomach-ache. He probably drank too much punch," said Selma smiling.

Coach looked at her and smiled. "Enjoy the dance," he said and nodding at Sal, he wandered away.

Sal smiled at Selma and drew her into another dance. "Never a dull moment," he said.

Selma gazed into his eyes and smiled at him. "You should be used to it in your job," she returned.

Sal laughed, "You maybe right," he agreed. "We make the perfect pair."

"Yes, we do," agreed Selma snuggling closer to Sal and laying her cheek against his shoulder. "It is a beautiful night," thought Selma. "Yes, it is," thought Sal in return.

It was the early hours of the morning before the band wrapped up with a final song. Some of the couples were headed out for an early breakfast, but Selma and Stacy decided not to join them. They had a busy schedule for the next week and decided rest was better than breakfast. Sal and Micky instructed Nelson to drive to the Mase home. Everyone was asleep in the house when they arrived. Sal opened the door quietly and led the way into the living room.

Both guys pulled their girls close for a goodnight kiss. After a pleasant interlude for both couples, Sal and Micky said good night and departed. Selma and Stacy made their way to their rooms. "I am so glad we have become friends," said Stacy softly, before she began to close her door. "I had more fun tonight than I did at my high-school prom."

"I'm glad we are friends, too," said Selma. "It made my prom night better, by having you there, also." The girls said goodnight and entered their rooms. Selma was careful not to wake Joyce, who was sleeping soundly.

The next morning, Selma was awakened from a sound sleep by the ringing of her phone.

"Hello," said Selma sleepily.

"Hello, Selma, I'm sorry to call so early. This is Alex Avorn."

"Mr. Avorn," said Selma suddenly wide awake. She glanced at the clock. It showed 10'o clock.

"It's not so early," said Selma.

"It is for after prom night," said Alex. "The reason I called is I have several things I need to discuss with you."

"Okay," said Selma. She looked over at the bed. Joyce was gone. She must have awakened earlier and was careful not to wake Selma.

"To start, I need to explain why Mariam will not be able to attend your graduation. It would be a security nightmare. I can't take a chance with Mariam so far along in her pregnancy."

"I understand. I had no idea you were even thinking about coming," said Selma.

"Mariam wanted to come, but we compromised," explained Alex.

"Compromised," echoed Selma confused.

"If it is okay with you, Brenda will attend. She will video tape the graduation so we can watch it later at home," said Alex.

"I don't mind at all," said Selma. "Do you think she could make me a copy while she is at it?"

Alex laughed. "I'll be sure to mention it to her. I have some other news, also. I spoke with your Aunt Phebe. She asked for you not to buy a wedding dress. She is bringing your mother's and your grandmother's wedding dresses with her so you can use the one you like best. I am sending a car for her and her family the day before your graduation. I am making a sixth- floor apartment in Avorn Building available for them while they are here. They will be staying the rest of the week and through your wedding. They will return to

Cendera after the hearing to adopt the children. We want to show the Judge that the children have a good back up system if it is needed," concluded Alex.

Selma stood speechless. "I don't know what to say. If I was there, I would give you a hug. You have solved all of my dilemma's in one sweep," said Selma. "Thank you."

Alex laughed. "If there is anything else, I can do to help, let me know."

After saying thank you once more, Selma and Alex hung up the phones. Selma jumped up and hurried to shower and dress. She had to talk to Stacy and tell her about the dresses.

Alex looked up as Sal and Micky entered his office. "I didn't expect to see either of you this morning," said Alex with a smile.

"We decided going to work was better than going shopping," said Micky.

"If you are talking about wedding dresses, Selma's aunt is taking care of them," said Alex. "There is one thing you can help me with." Alex looked at them thoughtfully.

Sal and Micky looked at Alex expectantly. "Selma's two young cousins will be with her Aunt Phebe. I thought I would purchase something to keep them occupied while they are here. Do you have any suggestions?"

Sal and Micky looked thoughtful. "The children these days seem to like those handheld video games. Selma and I just bought some for Jerry and Joyce," said Sal.

Alex nodded. "I'll send Lynn after some," he said.

"Tell her to get extra batteries. They use them up pretty fast," said Micky.

Alex nodded and made a note.

"While Selma's aunt is here, we need to take them to see where our homes are being built. Would you and Mariam like to see how our homes are progressing?" asked Sal.

Alex thought for a minute, then he nodded. "I think Mariam would like to see how Avorn Acres is progressing," said Alex. "She would like to get out and Avorn Acres is about the safest place to visit these days."

Since Alex did not seem to need them, Sal and Micky left. Alex promised to call them if anything came up.

"It was smooth, the way you convinced Alex to bring Mariam to Avorn Acres," said Micky.

"I will have to let Leo know so he can inform the people in charge of the statue. They need to know when to expect Alex and Mariam to be there, so they can be ready," said Sal.

At the Mase home, Selma entered the kitchen to find Joyce and Stacy sitting at the table talking while Stacy ate a late breakfast.

"Good morning," said Selma happily.

"Stacy smiled at her. You look awful happy this morning," she remarked.

"It's a beautiful day," said Selma. "I have had a call from Alex Avorn."

"Oh," Stacy said. "What did Mr. Avorn have to say?"

"He said my aunt and her family will be here the day before my graduation. They are going to stay until after the adoption hearing," said Selma.

"I know you will be glad to see them," remarked Stacy.

"That's not the best part," said Selma. "My aunt is bringing my mother's and my grandmother's wedding dresses with her. We won't have to go shopping for dresses."

Stacy didn't look enthusiastic about not going shopping.

Selma smiled. I have pictures of both ladies in their wedding dresses. You can look at them. If you don't like either of them, we can go shopping for you. I really love my mother's dress, but my grandmother's dress is a classic. So, I will be happy with either dress," said Selma.

Stacy smiled in relief. "I would like to see the pictures before I decide," she said.

"Okay," agreed Selma as she poured herself a cup of coffee and snagged a couple of pieces of toast to eat.

After eating, Selma, Stacy and Joyce went to Selma's room to look at pictures.

"Where is Jerry?" asked Selma.

"Grandad took him to work, at the store, with him," said Joyce. "Jerry wanted to go with him, and Grandad said it would do him good to get away from all of these females for a while."

Selma and Stacy laughed. "He will have a good time learning about the store," commented Selma.

Selma pulled her album from a box in her closet. They sat on the bed and started looking through it. When they came to Selma's grandmother's wedding photo, Stacy caught her breath in delight. "It's beautiful," whispered Stacy. Selma turned a few pages and produced a picture of her mother's wedding. Stacy agreed it was nice, but Selma could tell she liked the older dress more.

"Do you think they will fit?" asked Stacy gazing at the grandmother's photo longingly.

"If they need any small adjustments, My Aunt Phebe can fix them. She is a fantastic seamstress," said Selma.

"Great," said Stacy. "We don't have to go shopping. What else do we have to do?"

"I think we are covered for now. Why don't I call and see if we can take my brothers to visit the zoo? I'm sure Joyce would like a trip to the zoo. Joyce nodded, enthusiastic about the proposed treat.

Selma took out the telephone number for the antique shop owned by Marie Dolan and her brother and called the shop.

"Hello," answered a male voice.

"May I speak with Marie Dolan, please. Tell her Selma Dolan is calling," said Selma.

There was a short silence, then a female voice answered.

"Hello, this is Marie Dolan."

"Marie, this is Selma. I would like to meet my brothers. Would you and the boys like to meet me and some friends after church tomorrow? I thought I could treat us all to a trip to the zoo."

"What friends?" asked Marie cautiously.

"It would be me and my fiancée, my two adopted children, my friend Stacy and her fiancée," said Selma.

"I didn't know you had any kids," said Marie.

"Like I said, they are adopted. My daughter is 9 and my son is 12. I would really like to meet you and my brothers. Do you think they would like a trip to the zoo?" asked Selma.

Marie paused for a minute. "I think the boys would like a trip to the zoo very much," said Marie.

"Good, we will pick you up at 1:30. Do you want us to pick you up at the store or at home?" asked Selma.

"The store would be best," said Marie.

"Okay, we will see you tomorrow," said Selma.

Selma hung up the phone and turned to Joyce and Stacy. "We need a van. Our car is not big enough and we can not keep borrowing the Avorn limo," said Selma.

"I hear the guys in the kitchen. Why don't we see if they have any ideas about larger transportation?" remarked Stacy.

They went into the kitchen and found Sal and Micky raiding the refrigerator. Sal came over and gave Joyce a hug and Selma a kiss. Micky was quick to claim a kiss from Stacy.

"We are going to the zoo tomorrow," said Joyce happily.

"We are?" said Sal smiling as he looked at Selma.

Selma nodded. "I hope you don't mind. I was trying to find a way to spend some time with my brothers. I invited Marie and the boys. I didn't think she would let them go without her. She doesn't know me. I told her we would pick her and the boys up after church tomorrow." Selma smiled. "I thought there would be less chance of Albert trying to come along if we picked them up at the store. The only problem is our car will not hold everyone."

Sal looked at Micky and nodded. "We will see what we can do," said Sal as he and Micky started for the door to the garage. Sal stopped and gave Selma a quick kiss. "Don't worry. Micky and I will take care of everything."

Micky gave Stacy a kiss and followed Sal out the door.

CHAPTER 17

S al and Micky returned a couple of hours later with a small bus. They parked the bus in the Mase driveway and went in to bring Selma and Stacy out to see it.

"Where did you find this?" asked Selma.

"I borrowed it from Avorn Acres. It is used to transport the children in Avorn Acres to school and bring them home after school," explained Sal.

"It's perfect," said Stacy. "It will hold everyone easily."

"Why does Avorn Acres have its own bus to take the children to school?" asked Selma.

"Alex wants Avorn Acres to be a safe place for children. He wants them to be able to play and ride their bikes without worrying about someone snatching them. The only way to accomplish this is to control who can enter Avorn Acres. The public- school bus could have anyone riding it. It would be very easy for someone to sneak in on the bus. So, we have our own bus. The driver, and one guard, know everyone on the bus and they make sure no one gets left behind. It is safer for the children and gives peace of mind to the parents," concluded Sal.

"What happens if one of the residents decides to sell and leave Avorn Acres?" asked Stacy.

"It is written into the contract when they rent-to-own or buy a place, they can only sell to Avorn Security if they decide to move," explained Sal. "

Alex will not let anyone live in Avorn Acres until they have been thoroughly checked out," said Micky.

Alex has devoted himself to stopping the witch hunters and child trafficker's," said Sal. "He is very serious about it."

"I'm glad he is," said Selma hugging Joyce. "I'm glad someone will stand up and help the children," she said.

"Me, too," echoed Sal, Stacy and Micky.

Mrs. Mase drove up. She had been at the church getting it ready for services the next day. She gazed at the small bus in her drive and looked at Sal for an explanation.

"We are going to the zoo tomorrow," said Joyce.

Mrs. Mase nodded and smiled. "After church," said Mrs. Mase.

"Yes," agreed Selma. We are taking my brothers, so I can meet them and get to know them a little. Would you and Mr. Mase like to join us?"

"I think I will leave the zoo for you, young people. It is too much walking for me," said Mrs. Mase.

"If you change your mind, you are welcome to come along. We have plenty of room," said Sal.

"I can see you do," agreed Mrs. Mase as she took her things and with one last look at the bus, went inside the house.

On Tuesday night as Selma sat in the audience and waited for the graduation services to begin, she thought back over the last few days. The trip to the zoo had been a success. Selma had enjoyed meeting her brothers. They had seemed to enjoy meeting her, also. The setting, helped for a relaxed atmosphere. They all agreed to get together again soon. Selma's aunt and her family had arrived early the day before the graduation. Alex had sent Taylor Sarnes and Becky Semp in his limo to teleport them to Derring. They used Taylor's garage to teleport, so they would not be seen. With the help of Klark Aris, Taylor's dad, they managed to teleport the family safely. After they arrived, Sal and Micky had driven them to the Mase home. Aunt Phebe had shown the wedding dresses to Selma and Stacy. The girls loved the dresses. It had taken very few stitches to make them fit perfectly. Aunt Phebe had also brought along a flower girl dress for Joyce to wear.

Selma smiled thinking about how excited Joyce had been when she tried on her dress. Sal and Micky had taken Jerry to the shop where they had rented their tuxes and rented one for him to wear. He was going to stand as best man along with Sandy. It was all coming together nicely, thought Selma.

Selma looked around and waved at her family. They were sitting in the bleachers and waved at her excitedly. She saw Brenda with her camera already taking pictures. Selma looked forward as the graduation ceremony began. She listened to the speeches and felt proud of all she had accomplished to make it to this day. When her name was called, and she walked over to receive her certificate, the clapping and cheering was loud. Selma smiled and waved to her family. She went back to her seat to wait for the finish. They were all going to Andres to celebrate after the graduation was over.

The senior class marched out and Selma quickly turned in her gown and went to join her family. They were waiting with hugs and a quick kiss from Sal. Selma was surprised to see her dad and Marie, along with her brothers, had attended. She and Sal greeted them, and Sal invited them to join them at Andres. Selma looked at Sal curiously when he invited them along.

Sal smiled. "We may as well find away to get along with them," he said. "They are family."

"I suppose," said Selma. She was torn about the idea. She was still

leery of her dad, but she supposed she would have to put up with him
if she wanted a relationship with her brothers.

"It will all work out," said Sal giving her shoulder a squeeze.

Selma nodded and allowed Sal to lead her to the bus for the trip
to Avorn Security Building. Since school was out for the summer,
they were keeping the bus until they could purchase a van. When
they arrived, it took two elevator rides to get everyone to the first floor
and to Andres restaurant.

Andre was waiting for them. His crew had pulled several tables
together so everyone could sit at the same table. Lynn seated them
with a smile and congratulations for Selma. Selma flushed slightly at
all the attention she was getting. But, when she looked at the pride
and happiness in Jerry, Joyce, and Sal's faces, she was happy, also.

After they ordered and ate their meal, Andre came out with two
helpers. The helpers were carrying a large cake, it had a graduation
hat on it and the words, "CONGRATULATIONS SELMA," were
written on it. Everyone cheered and clapped when the cake was
placed on the table.

"Thank you, Andre," said Sal.

"You are welcome. Welcome to the Avorn family, Selma," said
Andre.

"Thank you," said Selma smiling at Andre. "The cake looks too
good to eat,"

Andre laughed. "It tastes better then it looks," he assured her. "I
have a graduation present for you from Andres," said Andre. He
handed Selma an envelope.

Selma opened the envelope and looked inside. She took out a gift
certificate. Selma raised misty eyes to smile at Andre. "Thank you,"
she said.

Andre nodded, well pleased with her reaction. Enjoy the cake,"
he said and left them so the waitresses could pass out slices of cake.

Sal leaned close to Selma. "What does it say?" he asked.

"It says I am to receive free meals from Andres for the next five years," said Selma. She placed the certificate back in its envelope and gave it to Sal for safe keeping.

Everyone enjoyed their cake and the leftover cake was placed in a container and given to Selma for later.

Selma told Aunt Phebe and Uncle Cameron goodnight. She gave Cecil and Clarence a hug. They took the elevator to the sixth floor where they were staying. Selma promised she would call her aunt the next day.

When they reached the Avorn garage, Selma bid her dad and Marie, along with Brandon and Bradley, good night and thanked them for coming. The rest of the group settled in the bus and headed for home.

It had been a long and exciting day. Selma was tired, but she wasn't sleepy.

They dropped Mr. and Mrs. Mase along with Jerry and Joyce at home. Selma and Sal went over to Stacy and Micky, after the children went inside.

"Would you mind keeping an eye on the children? Sal and I would like to go for a drive. I'm to wound up to sleep," Selma explained to Stacy.

"Micky will stay and help me keep them occupied. Go ahead and relax," said Stacy. Micky nodded his agreement.

"Thanks," said Sal as he helped Selma in the front seat of his car. They waved to Stacy and Micky, who watched them drive away.

"Where do you want to go?" asked Sal as they drove away.

"I want to go and see how much work has been done on our house and gaze off into the hills behind it," said Selma.

Sal smiled and turned the car toward Avorn Acres.

Sal pulled to a stop in front of the building site. Even though there had been considerable work done, all they could see was foundation work, with a lot of pipes sticking out of the ground.

Sal and Selma exited the car and looked up into the hills. Sal folded Selma into his arms and held her close as they gazed at the stars in the distance. "It's beautiful," said Selma on a sigh. "I can't wait until we have our porch to sit on and watch the stars at night,"

"I'm looking forward to those times myself," agreed Sal.

After watching the stars awhile longer and waving to the security guard as he drove by, Selma turned to face Sal. She raised her face for a kiss. When Sal ended the kiss, Selma sighed and snuggled into his arms.

"What is the sigh for?" asked Sal.

"I was just thinking how lucky we are. We have a wonderful life ahead of us. We have a great home, two wonderful children, and an unending love for each other. As my guardian angel says, everything is as it should be. We have surely solved Love's Dilemma."

"We are very lucky," agreed Sal. They turned and with Selma held close in his arms, they gazed into the hills at the stars.

THE END

Dear reader,

We hope you enjoyed reading *Love's Dilemma*. Please take a moment to leave a review, even if it's a short one. Your opinion is important to us.

Discover more books by Betty McLain at https://www.nextchapter. pub/authors/betty-mclain

Want to know when one of our books is free or discounted? Join the newsletter at http://eepurl.com/bqqB3H

Best regards,

Betty McLain and the Next Chapter Team

The story continues in:
Love's Familiar Face by Betty McLain

To read the first chapter for free, please head to:
https://www.nextchapter.pub/books/loves-familiar-face

ABOUT THE AUTHOR

With five children, ten grandchildren and six great-grandchildren, I have an extremely busy life, but reading and writing have always been a large and enjoyable part of my life. I've been writing since I was young. I wrote stories in notebooks and kept them private. They were all handwritten, because I was unable to type. We lived in the country, and I had to do most of my writing at night. My days were busy helping with my brothers and sister. I also helped Mom with the garden and canning food for our family. Even though I was tired, I still managed to get my thoughts down on paper at night.

When I married and began raising my family, I continued writing my stories while helping my children through school and then transitioning into their own lives and families. My sister was the only one to read my stories. She was very encouraging. When my youngest daughter started college, I decided to go to college myself. I had already completed my GED and only had to take a class to prepare for my college entrance tests. I passed with flying colors and even managed to get a partial scholarship. I took computer classes to learn typing. The English and literature classes helped me polish my stories.

I found that public speaking was not for me. I was much more comfortable with the written word, but researching and writing the speeches was helpful. I was able to use those skills to build a story.

I finished college with an associate degree and a 3.4 GPA. I earned several awards, including the President's List, Dean's List, and Faculty List. My school experience helped me gain more confidence with writing. I want to thank my college English professor for boosting my confidence with writing by telling me that I had a good imagination. She said I told an interesting story. My daughter, who is an excellent writer and has published many books, convinced me to publish some of my stories. She used her experience self-publishing to publish my stories for me. The first time I held one of my books and looked at my name on it as the author, I was proud. It was well received. Which encouraged me to continue writing and publishing. I have been building my library of books since then. I've also written and illustrated several children's books.

Being able to type my stories opened up a whole new world for me. Access to a computer helped me research anything I needed to know and expanded my ability to keep writing my books. Joining Facebook and making friends all over the world expanded my outlook considerably. I was able to understand many different lifestyles and incorporate them into my stories.

Ever heard the saying, watch out what you say, and don't make the writer mad. You may end up in a book being eliminated." Well, it is true. All of life is there to stimulate your imagination. It is fun to develop a story and to watch it come alive in your mind. When I get started, the stories almost write themselves; I just have to get all of it down as the ideas come to me, before they're gone.

I love knowing that the stories I have written are being read and enjoyed by others. It is awe-inspiring to look at the books and think, "I wrote that."

I look forward to many more years of creating and distributing my stories, and I hope the people reading my books are looking forward to reading them just as much as I enjoy writing them.

BOOKS BY BETTY MCLAIN

Rich Man's daughter

Dody

Love's Magic Series

Love's Magic Book 1

Love's Dream Book 2

Love's Time Book 3

Love's Reflection Book 4

Love's Call Book 5

Love's Prophesy Book 6

Love's Sight Book 7

Love's Answer Book 8

Love's Enemy Book 9

Love's Retaliation Book 10

Love's Obsession Book 11

Love's Memory Book 12

Love's Gamble Book 13

Love's Plea Book 14

Love's Promise Book 15

Love's Voice Book 16

Love's Helper Book 17

Love's Tuna Salad Book 18

Love's Vigilante Book 19

Love's Dilemma Book 20